THE SURGEON'S TALE
& OTHER STORIES

Two Free Lancer Press

THE SURGEON'S TALE
& OTHER STORIES

Cat Rambo
Jeff VanderMeer

Two Free Lancer Press
Seattle, Washington & Tallahassee, Florida

The Surgeon's Tale & Other Stories Copyright © 2007 Cat Rambo and Jeff Vander-Meer, with the following individual copyrights:

"The Surgeon's Tale," *Subterranean*, copyright © 2007 Cat Rambo and Jeff Vander-Meer
"The Dead Girl's Wedding March," *Fantasy Magazine*, copyright © 2006 Cat Rambo
"The Farmer's Cat," *Polyphony 5*, copyright © 2005 Jeff VanderMeer
"A Key Decides Its Destiny," *Say . . . What's the Combination?*, copyright © 2007 Cat Rambo
"The Strange Case of the Lovecraft Cafe," *Scattered, Covered, Smothered*, copyright © 2004 M.F. Korn, D.F. Lewis, and Jeff VanderMeer
"Three Sons" copyright © 2001 Cat Rambo

Special thanks to M.F. Korn and D.F. Lewis for permission to reprint "The Strange Case of the Lovecraft Cafe," as well as a big thank you to all of the publications in which these stories first appeared.

Cover design and illustration copyright © 2007 by James Owen
Interior illustrations copyright © 2007 by Kristine Dikeman

TWO FREE LANCER PRESS is:

Cat Rambo
http://www.kittywumpus.net
17315 NE 45th St. #142
Redmond, WA, 98052
spezzatura@gmail.com

Jeff VanderMeer
http://www.jeffvandermeer.com
POB 4248
Tallahassee, FL 32315
vanderworld@hotmail.com

To order more copies, visit our web page at:
http://www.kittywumpus.net/orders

Printed in the United States of America

For Wayne Rambo and Ann VanderMeer

Table of Contents

The Surgeon's Tale
Cat Rambo & Jeff VanderMeer

I.

Down by the docks, you can smell the tide going out—surging from rotted fish, filth, and the briny sargassum that turns the pilings a mixture of purple and green. I don't mind the smell; it reminds me of my youth. From the bungalow on the bay's edge, I emerge most days to go beach-combing in the sands beneath the rotted piers. Soft crab skeletons and ghostly sausage wrappers mostly, but a coin or two as well.

Sometimes I see an old man when I'm hunting, a gangly fellow whose clothes hang loose. As though his limbs were sticks of chalk, wired together with ulnar ligaments of seaweed, pillowing bursae formed from the sacs of decaying anemones that clutter on the underside of the pier's planking.

I worry that the sticks will snap if he steps too far too fast, and he will become past repair, past preservation, right in front of me. I draw diagrams in the sand flats to show him how he can safeguard himself with casings over his fragile limbs, the glyphs he should draw on his cuffs to strengthen his wrists. A thousand things I've learned here and at sea. But I don't talk to him—he will have to figure it out from my scrawls when he comes upon them. If the sea doesn't touch them first.

He seems haunted, like a mirror or a window that shows some landscape it's never known. I'm as old as he is. I wonder if I look like him. If he too has trouble sleeping at night. And why he chose this patch of sand to pace and wander.

9

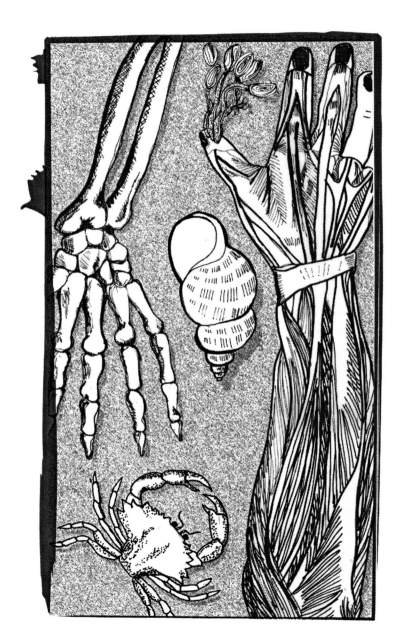

I will not talk to him. That would be like talking to myself: the surest path to madness.

I grew up right here, in my parents' cottage near the sea. Back then, only a few big ships docked at the piers and everything was quieter, less intense. My parents were Preservationists, and salt brine the key to their art. It was even how they met, they liked to tell people. They had entered the same competition—to keep a pig preserved for as long as possible using only essences from the sea and a single spice.

"It was in the combinations," my dad would say. "It was in knowing that the sea is not the same place here, here, or here."

My mother and father preserved their pigs the longest, and after a tie was declared, they began to see and learn from each other. They married and had me, and we lived together in the cottage by the sea, preserving things for people.

I remember that when I went away to medical school, the only thing I missed was the smell of home. In the student quarters we breathed in drugs and sweat and sometimes piss. The operating theaters, the halls, the cadaver rooms, all smelled of bitter chemicals. Babies in bottles. Dolphin fetuses. All had the milky-white look of the exsanguinated—not dreaming or asleep but truly dead.

At home, the smells were different. My father went out daily in the little boat his father had given him as a young man and brought back a hundred wonderful smells. I remember the sargassum the most, thick and green and almost smothering, from which dozens of substances could be extracted to aid in preservations. Then, of course, sea urchins, sea cucumbers, tiny crabs and shrimp, but mostly different types of water. I don't know how he did it—or how my mother distilled the essence—but the buckets he brought back did have different textures and scents. The deep water from out in the bay was somehow smoother and its smell was solid and strong, like the rind of some exotic fruit. Areas near the shore had different pedigrees. The sea grasses lent the water there, under the salt, the faint scent of glossy limes. Near the wrecks of iron-bound ships from bygone eras, where the octopi made their lairs, the water tasted of weak red wine.

"Taste this," my mother would say, standing in the kitchen in one of my father's shirts over rolled up pants and suspenders. Acid blotches spotted her hands.

I could never tell if there was mischief in her eye or just delight. Because some of it, even after I became used to the salt, tasted horrible.

I would grimace and my father would laugh and say, "Sourpuss! Learn to take the bitter with the sweet."

My parents sold the essence of what the sea gave them: powders and granules and mixtures of spices. In the front room, display cases stood filled with little pewter bowls glittering in so many colors that at times the walls seemed to glow with the residue of some mad sunrise.

This was the craft of magic in our age: pinches and flakes. Magic had given way to Science because Science was more reliable, but you could still find Magic in nooks and crannies, hidden away. For what my parents did, I realized later, could not have derived from the natural world alone.

People came from everywhere to buy these preservations. Some you rubbed on your skin for health. Some preserved fruit, others meat. And sometimes, yes, the medical school sent a person to our cottage, usually when they needed something special that their own ghastly concoctions could not preserve or illuminate.

My dad called the man they sent "Stinker" behind his back. His hands were stained brown from handling chemicals and the reek of formaldehyde was even in his breath. My mother hated him.

I suppose that is one reason I went to medical school—because my parents did not like Stinker. Does youth need a better excuse?

As a teenager, I became contemptuous of the kind, decent folk who had raised me. I contracted a kind of headstrong cabin fever, too, for we were on the outskirts of the city. I hated the enclosing walls of the cottage. I hated my father's boat. I even hated their happiness with each other, for it seemed designed to keep me out. When I came back from my studies at the tiny school created for the children of fishermen and sailors, the smell of preservatives became the smell of something small and unambitious. Even though poor, the parents of my schoolmates often went on long journeys into the world, had adventures beyond my ken. A few even worked for the old men who ran the medical school and the faltering mages' college. I found that their stories made me more and more restless.

When the time came, I applied to the medical school. They accepted me, much to the delight of my parents, who still did not understand my motivation. I would have to work for my tuition, my books, but that seemed a small price.

I remember a sense of relief at having escaped a trap. It is a feeling I do not understand now, as if my younger self and my adult selves were two entirely different people. But back then I could think only of the fact that I would be in the city's center, in the center of civilization. I would matter to more than just some farmers, cooks, fisherfolk, and the like. I would be saving lives from death, not just preserving dead things from decay.

The day I left, my father took me aside and said, "Don't become something separate from the work you do." The advice irritated me. It made no sense. But the truth is I didn't know what he meant at the time.

His parting hug, her kiss, though, were what sustained me during my first year of medical school, even if I would never have admitted it at the time.

The brittle-boned old man stands at the water's edge and stares out to sea. I wonder what he's looking at, so distant. The sargassum's right in front of him, just yards from the shore.

That's where I stare, where I search.

As a medical student, I lost myself in the work and its culture, which mainly meant sitting in the taverns boasting. I had picked up not just a roommate but a friend in Lucius, the son of a wealthy city official. We roamed the taverns for booze and women, accompanied by his friends. I didn't have much money, but I had a quick tongue and was good at cards.

Many long nights those first two years we spent pontificating over the cures we would find, the diseases we would bring to ground and eradicate, the herbs and mixes that would restore vitality or potency. We would speak knowingly about matters of demonic anatomy and supposed resurrection, even though as far as anyone knew, none of it was true. Anymore.

Lucius: They had golems in the old days, didn't they? Surgeons must have made them. Sorcerers wouldn't know a gall bladder from a spoiled wineskin.

Me: Progress has been made. It should be possible to make a person from some twine, an apple, a bottle of wine, and some cat gut.

Peter (Lucius' friend): A drunk person, maybe.

Lucius: You are a drunk person. Are you a golem?

Me: He's no golem. he's just resurrected. Do you remember when he began showing up? Right after we left the cadaver room.

Lucius: Why, I think you're right. Peter, are you a dead man?

Peter: Not to my knowledge. Unless you expect me to pay for all this.

Lucius: Why can't you be a resurrected woman? I have enough dead male friends.

During the days—oh marvel of youth!—we conquered our hangovers with supernatural ease and spent equal time in the cadaver room cutting up corpses and in classes learning about anatomy and the perilous weakness of the human body. Our myriad and ancient and invariably male instructors pontificated and sputtered and pointed their fingers and sometimes even donned the garb and grabbed the knife, but nothing impressed as much as naked flesh unfolding to show its contents.

And then there was the library. The medical school had been built around the library, which had been there for almost a thousand years before the school, originally as part of the mages' college. It was common knowledge, which is to say unsubstantiated rumor, that when the library had been built thaumaturgy had been more than just little pulses and glimpses of the fabric underlying the world. There had been true magic, wielded by a chosen few, and no one had need of a surgeon. But none of us really knew. Civilization had collapsed and rebuilt itself thrice in that span. All we had were scraps of history and old leather-bound books housed in cold, nearly airless rooms to guide us.

Lucius: If we were real surgeons, we could resurrect someone. With just a little bit of magic. Medical know-how. Magic. Magic fingers.

Me: And preservations.

Richard (another of Lucius' friends): Preservations?

Lucius: He comes from a little cottage on the—

Me: It's nothing. A joke. A thing to keep fetuses from spoiling until we've had a look at them.

Peter: What would we do with a resurrected person?

Lucius: Why, we'd put him up for the city council. A dead person ought to have more wisdom than a living one.

Me: We could maybe skip a year or two of school if we brought a dead person back.

Richard: Do you think they'd like it? Being alive again?

Lucius: They wouldn't really have a choice, would they?

Do you know what arrogance is? Arrogance is thinking you can improve on a thousand years of history. Arrogance is trying to do it to get the best of the parents who always loved you.

Me: There're books in the library, you know.

Lucius: Quick! Give the man another drink. He's fading. Books in a library. Never heard of such a thing.

Me: No, I mean—

Lucius: Next you'll be telling us there are corpses in the cadaver room and—

Richard: Let him speak, Lucius. He looks serious.

Me: I mean books on resurrection.

Lucius: Do tell . . .

For a project on prolonged exposure to quicksilver and aether, I had been allowed access to the oldest parts of the library—places where you did not know whether the footprints shown in the dust by the light of your shaking lantern were a year or five hundred years old. Here, knowledge hid in the dark, and you were lucky to find a little bit of it. I was breathing air breathed hundreds, possibly thousands, of years before by people much wiser than me.

In a grimy alcove half-choked with dust-filled spider webs, I found books on the ultimate in preservation: reanimation of dead matter. Arcane signs and symbols, hastily written down in my notebook.

No one had been to this alcove for centuries, but they *had* been there. As I found my halting way out, I noticed the faint outline of boot prints beneath the dust layers. Someone had paced before that shelf, deliberating, and I would never know their name or what they were doing there, or why they stayed so long.

Lucius: You don't have the balls.

Me: The balls? I can steal the balls from the cadaver room.

Richard: He can have as many balls as he wants!

Peter: We all can!

Lucius: Quietly, quietly, gents. This is serious business. We're planning on a grandiose level. We're asking to be placed on the pedestal with the greats.

Me: It's not that glorious. It's been done before, according to the book.

Lucius: Yes, but not for hundreds of years.

Peter: Seriously, you wonder why not.

Richard: I wonder why my beer mug's empty.

Peter: Barbarian.

Richard: Cretin.

Me: It seems easy enough. It seems as if it is possible.

One night, Lucius and I so very very drunk, trying too hard to impress, I boasted that with my secret knowledge of reanimation, my Preservationist background, and my two years of medical school, I could resurrect the dead, create a golem from flesh and blood. Human, with a human being's natural life span.

"And I will assist him," Lucius announced, finger pointed at the ceiling. "Onward!"

We stumbled out of the tavern's soft light, accompanied by the applause of friends who no doubt thought I was taking a piss—into the darkness of the street, and carried by drunkenness and the animating spirit of our youth, stopping only to vomit into the gutter once or maybe twice, we lurched our debauched way up the hill to the medical school, and in the shadows stole past the snoring old guard, into the cadaver room.

I remember the spark to the night, cold as it was. I remember the extravagant stars strewn across the sky. I remember the euphoria, being not just on a quest, but on a drunken quest, and together, best of friends in that moment.

If only we had stayed in that moment.

"Preservation is a neutral thing," my mother told me once. "It prolongs a state that already exists. It honors the essence of something."

She stood in the back room surrounded by buckets of pungent water when she said this to me. I think I was twelve or thirteen. She had a ladle and was stirring some buckets, sipping from others. Glints and sparkles came from one. Others were dark and heavy and dull. The floor, once white tile, had become discolored from decades of water storage. The bloody rust circles of the buckets. The hemorrhaging green-blue stains.

"But the essence of preservation," my mother said, "is that it doesn't last. You can only preserve something for so long, and then it is gone. And that's all right."

My father had entered the room just before she said this. The look of love and sadness she gave the two of us, me sitting, my father standing behind me, was so stark, so revelatory, that I could not meet her gaze.

Looking back at that moment, I've often wondered if she already knew our futures.

In the cadaver room, we picked a newly dead woman who had drowned in the sea. Probably the daughter of a fisherman. She lay exposed on the slab, all strong shoulders and solid breasts and sturdy thighs. Her ankles were delicate, though, as were the features of her face. She had frozen blue eyes and pale skin and an odd smile that made me frown and hesitate for a moment.

It will come as no surprise we chose her in part because her body excited me. Although Lucius' presence had helped me in this regard, women, for all our boasting, are not drawn to impoverished medical students. Even on those rare occasions, it had been in the dark and I had only had glimpses of a woman's naked form. The dissections of the classroom did not count; they would drive most men to celibacy if not for the resilience of the human mind.

"This one?" Lucius asked.

I don't know if he still thought this was a lark, or if he knew how serious I was.

"I think so," I said. "I think this is the one."

And, although I didn't know it, I did mean the words.

We stood there and stared at her. The woman reminded me of someone the more I stared. It was uncanny, and yet I could not think of who she looked like. So taken was I by her that I pushed her hair from her face.

Lucius nudged my shoulder, whispered, "Stop gawking. That guard might wake up or his replacement come by at any minute."

Together, we bundled her in canvas like a rug, stole past the guard, and, by means of a wagon Lucius had arranged—from a friend used to Lucius' pranks—we took her, after a brief stop at my apartment to pick up some supplies, to a secluded cove well away from the city. For you see, I meant to preserve her tethered in the water, in the sargassum near the rockline. It was a variation on an old preservation trick my mother had once shown a client.

The physical exertion was intense. I remember being exhausted by the time we hauled her out of the cart. Her body would not cooperate; there was no way for her not to flop and become unwound from the canvas at times. It added to the unreality of it all, and several times we collapsed into giggles. Perhaps we would have sobered up sooner if not for that.

Luckily the moon was out and Lucius had brought a lantern. By then, my disorganized thoughts had settled, and although I was still drunk I had begun to have doubts. But this is the problem with having an accomplice. If Lucius hadn't been there, I would like to think I'd have put a stop to it all. But I couldn't, not with Lucius there, not with the bond between us now. As for what kept Lucius beside me, I believe he would have abandoned me long before if not for a kind of jaded hedonism—the curiosity of the perpetually bored.

It was hard. I had to think of the woman as a receptacle, a vehicle, for resurrection, not the end result. We laid her out atop the canvas and I drew symbols on her skin with ink I'd daubed onto my fingers. Holding her right hand, I said the words I had found on the books, knowing neither their meaning nor their correct pronunciation. I rubbed preservatives into her skin that would not just protect her flesh while she lay amongst the sargassum but actually bring it back to health. I had to do some cutting, some surgery, near the end. An odd autopsy, looking for signs of the "mechanical defect" as one of my instructors used to say, that would preclude her reanimation. I cleared the last fluid from her lungs with a syringe.

By this time I could not tell you exactly what I was doing. I felt imbued with preternatural, instinctual knowledge and power, although I had neither. What I had were delusions of grandeur spurred on by alcohol and the words of my friends, tempered perhaps by memories of my parents' art.

Lucius held the lantern and kept muttering, "Oh my God" under his breath. But his tone was not so much one of horror as, again, morbid fascination. I have seen the phenomenon since. It is as if a mental list is being checked off on a list of unique experiences.

By the time I had finished, I knew the dead woman as intimately as any lover. We took her down to the sargassum bed and we laid her there, floating, tethered by one foot using some rope. I knew that cove. I'd swum in it since I was a child. People hardly ever came there. The sargassum was trapped; the tide only went out in the spring, when the path of the currents changed. The combination of the salt water, the preservatives I'd applied to her, and the natural properties of the sargassum would sustain her as she made her slow way back to life.

Except for the sutures, she looked as if she were asleep, still with that slight smile, floating on the thick sargassum, glowing from the emerald tincture that would keep the small crabs and other scavengers from her. She looked otherworldly and beautiful.

Lucius gave a nervous laugh. He had begun to sober up.

"Any suggestions on what we do next?" he said. His voice held disbelief.

"We wait."

"Wait? For how long? We've got classes in the morning. I mean, it's already morning."

21

"We wait for a day."

"Here? For a whole day?"

"We come back. At night. She'll still be here."

There's nothing in the nature of a confession that makes it any more or less believable. I know this, and my shadow on the beach knows it, or he would have talked to me by now. Or I would have talked to him, despite my misgivings.

I haven't seen Lucius in forty years. My shadow could be Lucius. It could be, but I doubt it.

II.

In the morning, for a time, neither Lucius nor I knew whether the night's events had been real or a dream. But the cart outside of our rooms, the deep fatigue in our muscles, and the blood and skin under our fingernails—this evidence convinced us. We looked at each other as if engaged in some uneasy truce, unwilling to speak of it, still thinking, I believe, that it would turn out to have been a hallucination.

We went to classes like normal. Our friends teased us about the bet, and I shrugged, gave a sheepish grin while Lucius immediately talked about something else. The world seemed to have changed not at all because of our actions and yet I felt completely different. I kept seeing the woman's face. I kept thinking about her eyes

Did the medical school miss the corpse? If so, they ignored it for fear of scandal. How many times a year did it happen, I've always wondered, and for what variety of reasons?

That night we returned to the cove, and for three nights more. She remained preserved but she was still dead. Nothing had happened. It appeared I could not bring her back to life, not even for a moment. The softly hushing water that rocked her sargassum bed had more life to it than she. Each time I entered a more depressed and numbed state.

"What's her name, do you think?" Lucius asked me on the third night.

He was sitting on the rocks, staring at her. The moonlight made her pale skin luminous against the dark green.

"She's dead," I said. "She doesn't have a name."

"But she had a name. And parents. And maybe a husband. And now she's here. Floating."

He laughed. It was a raw laugh. I didn't like what it contained.

On the afternoon of the first day, Lucius had been good-natured and joking. By the second, he had become silent. Now he seemed to have lost something vital, some sense of perspective. He sat on the rocks drawn in on himself, huddled for warmth. I hated his questions. I hated his attitude.

Even though it was I who pined for the woman, who so desperately wanted her to come to gasping life, to rise from the sargassum, reborn.

Everywhere I went, I saw those frozen blue eyes.

Once, before I left home, in that time when I was arguing with my parents almost every day, restless with their world and my place in it, there was a pause because each of us regretted something we had said.

Into this silence, my mother said, "You've got to know who you are, and even when you think you've been treated unfairly still *be* that person."

I said something sarcastic and stormed out of the cottage—to feel the salt air on my face, to look across the water toward distant, unseen shores.

I didn't know that I would one day find so much more so close to home.

⁓❊⁓

The fourth night Lucius refused to go with me.

"It's pointless," he said. "Not only that, it's dangerous. We shouldn't have done it in the first place. It's still a crime, to steal a body. Let it go. She'll be taken out to sea or rotting soon enough. Or put her out to sea yourself. Just don't mention it to me again."

In his face I saw fear, yes, but mostly awareness of a need for self-preservation. This scared me. The dead woman might have enthralled me, but Lucius had become my anchor at medical school.

"You're right," I told him. "I'll go one last time and put her out to sea."

Lucius smiled, but there was something wrong. I could feel it.

"We'll chalk it up to youthful foolishness," he said, putting his arm over my shoulders. "A tale to tell the grandchildren in thirty years."

She was still there, perfectly preserved, on that fourth night. But this time, rising from the sargassum, I saw what I thought was a pale serpent, swaying. In the next second, breath frozen in my throat, I realized I was staring at her right arm—and that it was moving.

I dashed into the water and to her side, hoping for what? I still don't know. Those frozen blue eyes. That skin, imperfect yet perfect. Her smile.

She wasn't moving. Her body still had the staunch solidity, the draining heaviness, of the dead. What I had taken to be a general awakening was just the water's gentle motion. Only the arm moved with any purpose—and it moved toward me. It sought me out, reaching. It touched my cheek as I stood in the water there beside her, and I felt that touch everywhere.

I spent almost an hour trying to wake her. I thought that perhaps she was close to full recovery, that I just needed to push things a little bit. But nothing worked. There was just the twining arm, the hand against my cheek, my shoulder, seeking out my own hand as if wanting comfort.

Finally, exhausted, breathing heavily, I gave up. I refreshed the preservation powders, made sure she was in no danger of sinking, and left her there, the arm still twisting and searching and alive.

I was crying as I walked away. I had been working so hard that it wasn't until that moment that I realized what had happened.

I had begun to bring her back to life.

Now if only I could bring her the rest of the way.

As I walked back up into the city, into the noise and color and sounds of people talking—back into my existence before her—I was already daydreaming about our life together.

The quality of the silence here can be extraordinary. It's the wind that does it. The wind hisses its way through the bungalow's timbers and blocks out any other sound.

The beach could be, as it sometimes is, crowded with day visitors and yet from my window it is a silent tableau. I can watch mothers with their children, building sandcastles, or beachcombers, or young couples, and I can create the dialogue for their lives. How many of them will make decisions that become the Decision? Who really recognizes when they've tipped the balance, when they've entered into a place from which there is no escape?

The old man knows, I'm sure. He has perspective. But the rest of them, they have no idea what awaits them.

For another week I went to her nightly, and each time the hand reached toward me like some luminous, five-petaled flower, grasping toward the moon. There was no other progress. Slowly, my hopes and daydreams turned to sleeplessness and despair. My studies suffered and I stammered upon questioning like a first year who couldn't remember the difference between a ligament and a radial artery. My friends stared at me and muttered that I worked too hard, that my brain had gone soft from overstudy. But I saw nothing but the woman's eyes, even when Lucius, without warning, while I was visiting her, moved out of our quarters. Leaving me alone.

I understood this, to some extent. I had become a bad roommate and, worse, a liability. But when Lucius began avoiding me in the halls, then I knew he had intuited I had gone farther, gone against his advice.

Finally, at the end of an anatomy class, I cornered him. He looked at me as if I were a stranger.

"I need you to come down to the water with me," I said.

"Why?" he said. "What's the point?"

"You need to see."

"What have you done?"

From Lucius' tone you would have thought I'd murdered someone.

"You just need to see. Please? For a friend?"

He gave me a contemptuous look, but said, "I'll meet you tonight. But I won't go down there with you. We meet there and leave separately."

"Thank you Lucius. Thank you so much."

I was so desperately grateful. I had been living with this secret in my head for almost a week. I hadn't been bathing. I hadn't been eating. When I did sleep, I dreamt of snow-white hands reaching for me from the sea. Hundreds of them, melting into the water.

⚜

I no longer think of my parents' bungalow as a trap. It's more of a solace—all of their things surround me. I can almost conjure them up from the smells alone. There is so much history here, of so many good things.

From the window, I can see the old man now. He seems restless, searching. Once or twice, he looked like he might come to the door, but he retreated and walked back onto the beach.

If I did talk to him, I don't know where I'd begin my story. I don't know if I'd wait for him to tell his or if mine would come out all in a mad rush, and there he'd be, still on the welcome mat, looking at this crazy old man, knowing he'd made a mistake.

Lucius at the water's edge that night. Lucius bent over in a crouch, staring at the miracle, the atrocity my lantern's light had brought to both of us. Lucius making a sound like a crow's harsh caw.

"It's like the movement of a starfish arm after you cut it off," he said. "It's no different from any corpse that flinches under the knife. Muscle memory."

"She's coming back to life," I said.

Lucius stood, walked over to me, and slapped me hard across the face. I reeled back, fell to one knee by the water's edge. It hurt worse than anything but the look in the woman's eyes.

Lucius leaned down to hiss in my ear: "This is an abomination. A mistake. You must let it go—into the sea. Or burn it. Or both. You must get rid of this, do you understand? For both of our sakes. And if you don't, I will come back down here and do it for you. Another thing: we're no longer friends. That can no longer be. I do not know you anymore." And, more softly: "You must understand. You must. This cannot be."

I nodded but I could not look at him. In that one whisper, my whole world had collapsed and been re-formed. Lucius had been my best friend; I had just not been his best friend. He was leaving me to my fate.

As I stood, I felt utterly alone. All I had left was the woman.

I looked out at her, so unbelievably beautiful floating atop the sargassum.

"I don't even know your name," I said to her. "Not even that."

Lucius was staring at me, but I ignored him and after a time he went away.

The woman's smile remained, as enigmatic as ever. Even now, I can see that smile, the line of her mouth reflected in everything around me—in the lip of a sea shell, or transferred to a child walking along the shore, or leaping into the sky in the form of a gull's silhouette.

Maybe things would have been different had I been close to any instructors, but outside of class, I never talked to them. I could not imagine going up to one of those dusty fossils, half-embalmed, and blurting out the details of my desperate and angst-ridden situation. How could they possibly relate? Nor did I feel as if I could go to my parents for help; that had not been an option in my mind for years.

Worst of all, I had never realized until Lucius began to avoid me that he had been my link to my few other friends. Now that Lucius had cast me adrift, no one wanted to talk to me. And, in truth, I was not good company. I don't know if I can convey the estrangement surrounding those days after I took Lucius to see her. I wandered through my classes like an amnesiac, speaking only when spoken to, staring out into nothing and nowhere. Unable to truly comprehend what was happening to me.

And every night: down to the sea, each time the ache in my heart telling me that what I believed, what I hoped, must have happened and she would be truly alive.

In that absence, in that solitary place I now occupied, I realized, slowly and with a mixture of fear and an odd satisfaction, that my interest in the woman's resurrection no longer came from hubris or scientific fascination. Instead it came from love. I was in love with a dead woman, and that alone began to break me down. For now I grieved for that which I had never had, to speculate on a life never lived, so that every time I saw that she had been taken from me, a part of my imagined life seemed to recede into the horizon.

"The arm grew stronger even as she did not," I would tell my fellow cast-away, both our beards gray and encrusted with barnacles and dangling crabs. I'm sure I would have practically had to kidnap him to get him into the bungalow, but once there I'd convince him to stay.

Over a cup of tea in the living room I'd say this as he looked at me, incredulous.

"Something in the magic I'd used," I'd say. "There was a dim glow to the arm. It even seemed to shimmer, an icy green. So I had succeeded, don't you see? I'd succeeded as well as I was ever going to. Magic might be almost utterly gone from the world now, but it still had a toe-hold when we were both young. Surely you remember, Lucius?"

In the clear morning light, the old man would say, "My name isn't Lucius and I think you've gone mad."

And he might be right.

Ultimately, the love in my heart led to my decision, not any fear of discovery. I couldn't bear the ache anymore. If she no longer existed, that ache would be gone. Foolish boys know no better. Everything is physical to them. But that ache is still here in my heart.

It was a clear night. I stole a boat from the docks and rowed my way to the hidden cove. She was there, of course, unchanged. I had with me jars of oil.

I had a hard time getting her from the bed of sargassum into the boat. I remember being surprised at her weight as I held her in my arms in the water for a time and cried into her hair, her hand caressing the back of my head.

After she was in the boat, I took it out to where the currents would bring it to deep water. I poured the oil all over her body. I lit the match. I stared into those amazing eyes one last time, then tossed the match onto the oil as I jumped into the sea. Behind me, I heard the whoosh of air and felt a rush of heat as flames engulfed the rowboat. I swam to shore without looking back. If I had looked back, I would have turned around, swum out to the burning boat, and let myself be immolated beside her.

As I staggered out of the water, I felt relief mixed with the sadness. It was over with. I felt I had saved myself from something I did not quite understand.

"What happened then," old man Lucius would say, intent on my story, forgetting the thread of his own.

"For three days, everything returned to a kind of normal," I'd tell him. "Or as normal as it could be. I slept. I went out with a couple of the first-years who didn't know you had abandoned me. I felt calm as a waveless sea."

"Calm? After all of that?"

"Perhaps I was in shock. I don't know."

"What happened after the third day?"

My guest would have to ask this, if I didn't tell him right away.

"What happened after the third day? Nothing much. The animated right arm of a dead woman climbed up the side of my building and crawled in through the window."

And with that, Lucius would be frozen in time, cup cantilevered toward his mouth, shock suffusing his face like honey crystals melting in tea.

I woke up with the arm beside me in bed. I tried to scream, but the hand closed gently over my mouth. The skin was smooth but smelled of brine. With an effort of will, I got up, pulled the arm away, and threw it back onto the bed. It lay there, twitching. There was sand under its fingernails.

I began to laugh. It was after midnight. I was alone in my room with a reanimated, disembodied arm.

Her arm. Her hand.

31

It had come to me from the depths of the sea, crawling across the sea floor like some odd creature in an old book.

What would you have done? I remembered Lucius' comment that the arm displayed the same mindless motion as a wounded starfish.

I took the arm downstairs and buried it in the backyard, weighed down with bricks and string like an unwanted kitten. Then I went back to bed, unable to sleep, living with a constant sense of terror the next day.

The next night, the arm was in my room again, last remnant of my lost love.

I buried it three more nights. It came back. I tossed it into the sea. It came back. I became more creative. I mixed the arm in with the offal behind a butcher's shop, holding my nose against the stench. It came back, smeared with blood and grease. I slipped it into an artist's bag at a coffee shop. It came back, mottled with vermillion and umber paint. I tried to cut it to pieces with a bone saw. It reconstituted itself. I tried to burn it, but, of course, it would not burn.

Eventually, I came to see it meant me no harm. Not really. Whatever magic bound it, it did not seek revenge. I hadn't killed the woman. I just hadn't brought her fully back to life. In return she hadn't come fully back to me.

"So then you kept it locked in a box in your room, you say?"

"Yes," I would tell my shadow. "There was no real danger of discovery—no one came to visit me anymore. And I rarely went to classes. I was searching for answers, for a way out. You have to understand, I was in an altered state by then."

"Of course."

A sip of tea and no inclination to divulge his own secrets.

The sea beyond the window is the source of the biggest changes for me now. It goes from calm to stormy in minutes. The color of it, the tone of the waves, varies by the hour. Over the months, it brings me different things: the debris of a sunken ship, a cornucopia of jellyfish, and, of course, strands of sargassum washed up from the bay.

"I was insane," I tell him.

"Of course you were. With grief."

Youth is a kind of insanity. It robs you of experience, of perspective, of history. Without those, you are adrift.

Back to the libraries I went, and back again and again. But it was as if the floors had been swept and I could not trace my own footprints. In those echoing halls, I found every book but the one that would have helped me. Had my long-ago counterpart, standing there deliberating, thought about stealing the book? No matter now, but I found myself reliving the moment when I had slid the tome back into the stacks rather than hiding it in my satchel with at first horror and then resignation.

I even visited the remnants of the mage's college, following the ancient right wing of the library until it dissolved into the even more crumbling walls of that venerable institution. All I found there was a ruined amphitheater erupting in sedgeweeds, with a couple dozen students at the bottom, dressed in black robes. They were being lectured at by a man so old he seemed part of the eroded stones on which he sat. If magic still remained in the world, it did not exist in this place.

All I had left were the more modern texts and the memory of a phrase among the signs and symbols I had used to animate the arm: "Make what you bring back your own."

Each time I took the arm out of the box, it came garlanded with thoughts I did not want but could not make go away. Each time, I unraveled a little more. Dream and reality blended like one of my parents' more potent concoctions. Day became night and night became day with startling rapidity. I had hallucinations in which giant flowers became giant hands. I had visions of arms reaching from a turbulent, bloody sea. I had nightmares of wrists coated with downy hair and mold.

I stopped bathing entirely. I wore the same clothes for weeks. Her skin's briny taste filled my mouth no matter what cup I drank from. Her eyes stared from every corner.

"What did you do then?" my guest would prod once again. He'd have finished his tea by now and he would be wanting to leave, but ask despite himself.

"Don't you know, Lucius?" I'd reply. "Don't you remember?"

"Tell me anyway," he'd say, to humor the other crazy old man.

"One night, sick with weariness, with heartache, I took the arm to the medical school's operating theater and performed surgery on myself."

A rapid intake of breath. "You did?'

"No, of course not. You can't perform that kind of surgery on yourself. Impossible. Besides, the operating theater has students and doctors in it day and night. You can't sneak into an operating theater the way you sneak into a cadaver room. Too many living people to see you."

"Oh," he'd say, and lapse into silence.

Maybe that's all I'd be willing to tell my Lucius surrogate. Maybe that's the end of the story for him.

One night, sick with weariness, with heartache, I took the arm to the medical school's operating theater and performed surgery on myself.

It wasn't the operating theater and I wasn't alone. No, my friend was with me the whole time.

Me, tossing the proverbial pebbles from some romantic play at the window of Lucius' new apartment one desperate, sleepless night. Hissing as loud as I could: "Lucius! I know you're in there!"

More pebbles, more hissing, and then he, finally, reluctantly, opening the window. In the light pouring out, I could see a woman behind him, blonde and young, clutching a bed sheet.

Lucius stared down at me as if I were an anonymous beggar.

"Come down, Lucius," I said. "Just for a moment."

It was a rich neighborhood, not where one typically finds starving medical students. Not the kind of street where any resident wants a scene.

"What do you want?" he whispered down at me.

"Just come down. I won't leave until you do."

Again, that measured stare. Suddenly I was afraid.

He scowled and closed the window, but a minute later he stood in the shadow of the doorway with me, his hair disheveled, his eyes slits. He reeked of beer.

"You look like shit," he said to me. "You look half-dead." Laughed at his own joke. "Do you need money? Will that make you go away?"

Even a few days earlier that would have hurt me, but I was too far gone to care.

"I need you to come down to the medical school."

"Not in a million years. We're done. We're through."

I took the arm out of my satchel and unwrapped it from the gauze in which it writhed

Lucius backed away, against the door, as I proffered it to him. He put out his hand to push it away, thought better of it.

"She came back to me. I burned the body, but the arm came back."

"My god, what were you *thinking*? Put it away. Now."

I carefully rewrapped it, put it back in the satchel. The point had been made.

"So you'll help me?"

"No. Take that abomination and leave now."

He turned to open the door.

I said: "I need your help. If you don't help, I'll go to the medical school board, show them the arm, and tell them your role in this." There was a wound in me because of Lucius. Part of me wanted to hurt him. Badly.

Lucius stopped with his hand on the doorknob, his back to me. I knew he was searching furiously for an escape.

"You can help me or you can kill me, Lucius," I said, "but I'm not going away."

Finally, his shoulders slumped and he stared out into the night.

"I'll help, all right? I'll help. But if you ever come here again after this, I'll . . . "

I knew exactly what he'd do, what he might be capable of.

My parents had a hard life. I didn't see this usually, but at times I would catch hints of it. Preservation was a taxing combination of intuition, experimentation, and magic. It wasn't just the physical cost—my mother's wrists aching from hundreds of hours of grinding the pestle in the mortar, my father's back throbbing from hauling buckets out of the boat nearly every day. The late hours, the dead-end ideas that resulted in nothing they could sell. The stress of going out in a cockleshell of a boat in seas that could grow sullen and rough in minutes.

No, preservation came with a greater cost than that. My parents aged faster than normal—well-preserved, of course, even healthy, perhaps, but the wrinkles gathered more quickly on their faces, as did the age spots I thought were acid blotches and that they tried to disguise or hide. None of this was normal, although I could not know it at the time. I had no other parents to compare them to or examine as closely.

Once, I remember hearing their voices in the kitchen. Something in their tone made me walk close enough to listen, but not close enough to be seen.

"You must slow down," she said to him.

"I can't. So many want so much."

"Then let them *want*. Let them go *without*."

"Maybe it's an addiction. Giving them what they want."

"I want you with me, my dear, not down in the basement of the Preservation Guild waiting for a resurrection that will never come."

"I'll try . . . I'll be better . . . "

" . . . Look at my hands . . . "

" . . . I love your hands . . . "

" . . . so dry, so old . . . "

"They're the hands of someone who works for a living."

"Works too hard."

"I'll try. I'll try."

III.

I'll try. I'll try. To tell the rest of the story. To make it to the end. Some moments are more difficult than others.

When Lucius discovered what I planned to do, he called me crazy. He called me reckless and insane. I just stood there and let him pace like a trapped animal and curse at me. It hardly mattered. I was resolute in my decision.

"Lucius," I said. "You can make this hard or you can make this easy. You can make it last longer or you can make it short."

"I wish I'd never known you," he said to me. "I wish I'd never introduced you to my friends."

In the end, my calm won him over. Knowing what I had to do, the nervousness had left me. I had reached a state so beyond that of normal human existence, so beyond what even Lucius could imagine, that I had achieved perfect clarity. I can't explain it any other way. The doubt, in that moment, had fallen from me.

"So you'll do it?" I asked again.

"Let's get on with it," Lucius growled, and I had a fleeting notion that he would kill me rather than do it when he said, "But not at the operating theater. That's madness. There's a place outside the city. A house my father owns. You will wait for me there. I'll get the tools and supplies I need from the school."

Desperation, lack of sleep, and a handful of pills Lucius had been able to steal served as my only anesthetics. I had no idea, even with Lucius' help, even with my knowledge of preservation powders, if it would work. In effect, it might have been the equivalent of an assisted suicide attempt. I lay spread out on the long dining room table of that house while Lucius prepared his instruments, knowing that these minutes, these seconds, might be my last among the living.

The pain was unbelievable. I jolted in and out of consciousness to hear Lucius panting like a dog. Lucius sawing. Lucius cursing. Lucius cutting and suturing and weeping, blood everywhere, me delirious and singing an old nursery rhyme my mother had taught me, Lucius bellowing his distress in counterpoint.

"I never want to see you again," he gasped in my ear as he finished up. "Never."

I smiled up at him and reached out with my good arm to touch his bloodstained face, to say "It's all right, Lucius. It's going to be okay." And: "Thank you." The pain burned through my skull like a wildfire. The pain was telling me I was alive.

When Lucius was done, he slumped against the side of the table, wiping at his hands, mumbling something I couldn't understand. It wasn't important. All I knew was that my own right arm had been consigned to the morgue and the woman's arm had replaced my own.

Lucius saw to it that I got back to my apartment, although all I have are vague flashbacks to the inside of a cart and a painful rolling sensation. Afterwards I spent two feverish weeks in bed, the landlady knocking on the door every day, asking for the rent. I think Lucius visited me to clean and check the wound, but I can't be sure.

My memory of that time comes and goes in phases like the tide.

In the end, the same sorcery that animated the woman's arm saved me. Over time, I healed. Over time, my new arm learned to live with me. I worried at first about gangrene in the place where the arm met my flesh, but I managed to prevent that. In the mornings, I woke with it as though it was a stranger I had brought home from a tavern. Eventually, it would wake me, stroking my forehead and touching my lips so delicately that I would groan my passion out into its palm.

It was the beginning of my life, in a way. A life in exile, but a life nonetheless, with a new partner. Lucius had helped me see to that.

So it was that when I went back to my parents' bungalow, I had a purpose and a plan.

They met me at the door and hugged me tight, for they hadn't heard from me in months and I was gaunt, pale.

I did not have to tell them everything. Or anything. I tried to hide the new arm from them, but it reached out for my mother as though gathering in a confidante. What did it say to her, woman to woman? What secrets did it spell into her hands? I had to look away, as though intruding on their conversation.

"What will you do?" my father asked.

As my mother held my new arm, he had run a fingertip across it, come away with a preserving dust.

I wanted to say that I had come to ask his advice, but the truth was I had only returned after I had settled my fate. In the days, the hours, before everything had become irrevocable, I hadn't sought their counsel. And he knew that, knew it in a way that filled his eyes with bewilderment, like a solution of cobalt chloride heated to its purest color.

"What will I do?" I knew, but I didn't know if I could tell them.

My father had his hand on my shoulder, as if needing support. My mother released the arm and it returned to me and tucked its hand into my pocket, taking refuge. She had not yet said a word to me.

I told them: "I've signed on as a ship's doctor. I've enough experience for that. My ship leaves for the southern islands in three days." The arm stirred, but only barely, like an eavesdropper that has overheard its own name.

Lucius' father owned the ship. It had been Lucius' last favor to me, freely and eagerly given. "As far from the city as possible," he said to me. "As far and for as long as possible."

My father looked crushed. My mother only smiled bravely and said, "Three days is not enough, but it will have to do. And you will write. And you will come back."

Yes, I would come back, but those three days—during which I would tell them everything, sometimes defiant, sometimes defeated and weeping—were my last three days with them.

Even in the shallow water near the bungalow, you learn to find shapes in shadow, if you look long enough. Staring into deep water as it speeds past and sprays white against the prow of a large ship, the wind lacerating your face, you see even more.

But I never saw *her*. I never saw her. I don't know why I expected to, and yet on all of the hundreds of voyages I took as a ship's doctor, I always looked. The sailors say mermaids live down there, with scaly hair and soft fingertips and cold, clammy kisses. I cared for none of that. I yearned to see her face by some strange necromancy, her blue eyes staring up at me through the ocean's darker blue.

Worse yet, whether on deck or in my cabin, whether during ferocious, stomach-churning storms or trying to save a man with a jagged piece of the deck forced through his sternum, I wanted a dead woman to tell the story of her life. I wanted to know if she had been a sister, a niece, a granddaughter. I wanted to know if she played with kittens or tormented them. Did she brew tea or drink coffee? Did she have an easy sense of humor? Was her laugh thin or full? How did she walk? What did she like to wear? So many questions came to me.

Because I had no idea of her personality, I imagined her, probably wrongly, as my double: embarrassed by her parents' eccentricities, a little amazed to find herself touched by life and led as though by the nose to this point of existence, this moment when I searched a hundred flavors of water for her smile.

It wasn't a moot point. I experienced the sweet agony of living with a part of her every day. At first, I had little control over it, and it either flopped loosely at my side, uncooperative, or caused much trouble for me by behaving eccentrically. But, over time, we reached an accord. It was more skillful than I at stitching a wound or lancing a boil. The arm seemed to so enjoy the task that I wondered if the woman had been a thwarted healer or something similar—an artist of the domestic, who could sew or cook, or perform any arcane household task.

Sometimes, at night, it would crawl outside the counterpane, to the limits of its span, and lie in the cold air until the shivers woke me and forced me to reclaim it. Then I would besiege it with the warmth of my own flesh until it succumbed and became part of me again.

"Did you enjoy being a ship's doctor?" my guest would ask, if only to change the topic, and I would be grateful.

"It was boring and exhausting," I would say. "Sailors can injure themselves in a thousand different ways. There's only so much medicine you can carry on a ship."

"But did you enjoy it?"

"When it was busy, I would get pleasure from doing good and necessary work."

Keeping busy is important. My parents taught me that the utility of work was its own reward, but it also fills up your mind, gives you less time to think.

"Sounds like it wasn't half-bad," he'd say, like someone who didn't know what I was talking about.

Would I tell him the rest? Would I tell him about the times on the docks or at sea that I saw the pale white of drowning victims laid out in rows and immediately be back in the cadaver room? That some part of me yearned for that white dead flesh? That when I slept with women now it must be in the dark so that the soft yet muscular whiteness of them would not interfere with the image in my head of a certain smile, a certain woman. That I tried to fall in love with so many women, but could not, would not, not with her arm by my side.

In time, I gained notoriety for my skills. When docked, sailors from other ships would come to me for bandaging or physicking, giving themselves over to my mismatched hands. My masculinity had never seemed brutish to me, but laid against her delicate fingers, I could not help but find myself unsubtle. Or, at least, could not help but believe she would find them so. And, indeed, the arm never touched the other hand if it could avoid it, as if to avoid the very thought of its counterpart.

I settled into the life easily enough—every couple of years on a new ship with a new crew, headed somewhere ever more exotic. Soon, any thought of returning to the city of my birth grew distant and faintly absurd. Soon, I gained more knowledge of the capriciousness of sea than any but the most experienced seaman. I came to love the roll of the decks and the wind's severity. I loved nothing better than to reach some new place and discover new peoples, new animals, new cures to old ailments. I survived squalls, strict captains, incompetent crews, and boardings by pirates. I wrote long letters about my adventures to my parents, and sometimes their replies even caught up to me, giving me much pleasure. I also wrote to Lucius once or twice, but I never heard back from him and didn't expect to; nor could I know for sure my letters had made it into his hands, the vagaries of letters-by-ship being what they are.

In this way thirty years passed and I passed with them, growing weather-beaten and bearded and no different from any other sailor. Except, of course, for her arm.

At a distant river port, in a land where the birds spoke like women and the men wore outlandishly bright tunics and skirts, a letter from my mother caught up with me. In it, she told me that my father had died after a long illness, an illness she had never mentioned in any of her other letters. The letter was a year old.

I felt an intense confusion. I could not understand how a man who in my memory I had said goodbye to just a few years before could now be dead. It took awhile to understand I had been at sea for three decades. That somewhere in the back of my mind I had assumed my parents would live forever. I couldn't accept it. I couldn't even cry.

Six months later, slowly making my way back to my mother, another letter, this time from a friend of the family. My mother had died and been laid next to my father in the basement of the Preservation Guild.

It felt as if the second trauma had made me fully experience the first. All I could think of was my father. And then the two of them working together in their bungalow.

I remember I stood on the end of a rickety quay in a backwater port reading the letter. Behind me the dismal wooden shanty town and above explosions of green-and-blue parrots. The sun was huge and red on the horizon, as if we were close to the edge of the world.

Her hand discarded the letter and reached over to caress my hand. I wept silently.

Five years later, I tired of life at sea—it was no place for the aging—and I returned home. The city was bigger and more crowded. The medical school carried on as it had for centuries. The mages' college had disappeared, the site razed and replaced with modern, classroom-filled buildings.

I stored my many trunks of possessions—full of rare tinctures and substances and oddities—at a room in a cheap inn and walked down to my parents' bungalow. It had been abandoned and boarded-up. After two days, I found the current owner. He turned out to be a man who resembled the Stinker of my youth in the fatuousness of his smile, the foulness of his breath. This new Stinker didn't want to sell, but in the end I took the brass key, spotted with green age, from him and the bungalow was mine.

Inside, beneath the dust and storm damage, I found the echoes of my parents' preservations—familiar fond splotches across the kitchen tiles—and read their recipes in the residue.

From these remnants, what they taught me of their craft, and the knowledge I brought back from my travels, I now make my modest living. These are not quite the preservations of my youth, for there is even less magic in the world now. No, I must use science and magic in equal quantities in my tinctures and potions, and each comes with a short tale or saying. I conjure these up from my own experience or things my parents told me. With them, I try to conjure up what is so easily lost: the innocence and passion of first love, the energy and optimism of the young, the strange sense of mystery that fills midnight walks along the beach. But I preserve more prosaic things as well—like the value of hard work done well, or the warmth of good friends. The memories that sustain these concoctions spring out of me and through my words and mixtures into my clients. I find this winnowing, this release, a curse at times, but mostly it takes away what I do not want or can no longer use.

Mine is a clandestine business, spread by word-of-mouth. It depends as much on my clients' belief in me as my craft. Bankers and politicians, merchants and landlords hear tales of this strange man living by himself in a Preservationists' bungalow, and how he can bring them surcease from loneliness or despair or the injustice of the world.

Sometimes I wonder if one day Lucius will become one of my clients and we will talk about what happened. He still lives in this city, as a member of the city council, having dropped out of medical school, I'm told, not long after he performed the surgery on me. I've even seen him speak, although I could never bring myself to walk up to him. It would be too much like talking to a ghost.

Still, necessity might drive me to him as it did in the past. I have to fill in with other work to survive. I dispense medical advice to the fisherfolk, many driven out of work by the big ships, or to the ragged urchins begging by the dock. I do not charge, but sometimes they will leave a loaf of bread or fish or eggs on my doorstep, or just stop to talk. My life is simple now.

Over time, I think I have forgiven myself. My thoughts just as often turn to the future as the past. I ask myself questions like *When I die, what will she do?* Will the arm detach itself, worrying at the scar line with sharpened fingernails, leaving only the memory of my flesh as the fingers pull it like an awkward crab away from my death bed? Is there an emerald core that will be revealed by that severance, a glow that leaves her in the world long after my passing? Will this be loss or completion?

For her arm has never aged. It is as perfect and smooth and strong as when it came to me. It could still perform surgery if the rest of me had not betrayed it and become so old and weak.

Sometimes I want to ask my mirror, the other old man, what lies beyond, and if it is so very bad to be dead. Would I finally know her then? Is it too much of a sentimental, half-senile fantasy, to think that I might see her, talk to her? And: have I done enough since that ecstatic, drunken night, running with my best friend up to the cadaver room, to have deserved that mercy?

One thing I have learned in my travels, one thing I know is true. The world is a mysterious place and no one knows the full truth of it even if they spend their whole life searching. For example, I am writing this account in the sand, each day's work washed away in time for the next, lost unless my counterpart has been reading it.

I am using my beloved's hand, her arm as attached to me as if we were one being. I know every freckle. I know how the bone aches in the cold and damp. I can feel the muscles tensing when I clench the purple stick and see the veins bunched at the wrist like a blue delta. A pale red birthmark on the heel of her palm looks like the perfect snail crossing the tide pool at my feet.

We never really knew each other, not even each other's names.

The Dead Girl's Wedding March

Cat Rambo

Once upon a time a dead girl lived with the other zombies in the caverns below the port of Tabat, in the city beneath that seaside town, the city that has no name. Thousands of years ago, the Wizard Sulooman plunged the city, buildings and all, into the depths of the earth, and removed its name, over some slight that no one but his ghost remembers. There life continues.

Some dead folk surrender to slumber, feeling that there is no point pretending an agenda for each day. A few, though, pace out their days in the way they once paced out their lives.

The only actual living things in the City of the Dead are the sleek, silver-furred rats that slip through its streets like reversed shadows. On a day there like any other day, a rat addressed the dead girl.

Her name was Zuleika, and she was dark-haired, dark-eyed, and smelled only faintly of the grave, because every evening she bathed in the river that flowed silently beneath her window.

"Marry me," the rat said. It stood upright on its back legs, its tail curled neatly around its feet.

She was pretending to eat breakfast. A pot steamed on the table. She poured herself a deliberate cup of chocolate before speaking.

"Why should I marry you?"

The rat eyed her. "To be sure," it admitted. "There's more in it for me than for you. Having a bride of your stature would increase mine, so to speak." It chuckled, smoothing its whiskers with a paw.

"I fear I must decline," she said.

She left the rat to console itself with muffins, and went went into the parlor where her father sat reading the same paper he read every morning, its pages black rectangles.

"I have had a marriage proposal," she told him.

He folded his paper and set it down, frowning. "From whom?"

"A rat, just now. At breakfast."

"What does he expect? A dowry of cheese?"

She remembered not liking her father very much when she was alive.

"I told him no," she said.

He reached for his paper again. "Of course you did. You've never been in love and never will be. There is no change in this city. Indeed, it would be the destruction of us all. Shut the door when you go out."

She went shopping, carrying a basket woven from the white reeds that line the river's banks.

Passing through a clutter of stalls, she fingered fabrics lying in drifts: sleepy soft velvet, watery charmeuse, suedes as tender as a mouse's ear. All in shades of black and gray, whites lying among them like discarded moonlight.

The rat sat on the table's edge.

"I can provide well for you," it said. "Fish guts from the docks of Tabat and spoiled meat from its alleyways. I would bring you the orchard's gleanings: squishy apricot and rotted peaches, apples brown as bone and flat as the withered breasts of a crone. I would bring you bits of ripe leather from the tannery, soaked in a soup of pigeon shit and water until they are soft as flesh."

"Why me?" she asked. "Have I given you reason to suspect I would accept your advances?"

It stroked its whiskers in embarrassment. "No," it admitted. "I witnessed you bathing in the river, and saw the touch of iridescence that gilds your limbs, like plump white cheeses floating in the water. I felt desire so strong that I pissed myself, as though my bones had turned to liquid and were flowing out of me. I *must* have you for my wife."

She looked around at the market she had visited each third day for as long as she had been dead. At the tables of wares that never changed but only endlessly rearranged their elements. Then back at the rat.

"You may walk with me," she said.

The rat hopped into the basket and they strolled along in silence. At length, he began to speak.

He told her of the rats of the city without a name, who have lived so long and so close to magic that it has seeped into their skin, their eyes, and down into their very guts. How they have seen their civilizations rise and fall over the centuries, and their sorcerers and magicians have learned cunning magics, only to see them torn away each time they re-descended into savagery. How the white-furred rat matrons ruled their current society, sending their swains out to gather them food, eating more and more, in order to gain greater and greater social weight.

"That is what first drew me to this idea," he said. "A human bride would have more weight than any of them. But then when I saw you, it seemed a meaningless and stale calculation."

She felt a thrill of warmth somewhere in her chest. Upon reflection she realized that it was an emotion that she had not felt before she died. It was part interest, and part intrigue, and part vanity, and part something else: a twinge of affection for this rat that promised to make her his world.

"There is no question," her father said. "This would bring change to the City."

"And?"

"And! Do you wish to destroy this place? We are held by the Wizard's spell – fixed in a moment when, dying because we cannot change, we do not die because we cannot change."

Zuleika frowned. "That makes no sense."

"That's because you're young."

"You have only forty years more than my own five thousand, three hundred and twelve. Surely when one considers the years I have lived, I can be reckoned an adult."

"You would think so, if you overlooked the fact that you will always be fifteen."

She stamped her foot and pouted, but centuries can jade even the most indulgent father. He sent for a Physician.

The Physician came with eager steps, for new cases were few and far between. He insisted on examining Zuleika from head to toe, and would have had her disrobe, save for her father's protest.

"She seems well enough to me," the Physician said in a disappointed tone.

"She believes she wishes to marry."

"Tut, tut," the Physician said in astonishment. "Well now. Love. And you wish this cured?"

"Before the contagion spreads any further or drives her to actions imperiling us all."

Zuleika said nothing. She was well aware she was not in love with the rat. But the idea of change had seized her like a fever.

The Physician overlaid her scalp with a netting of silver wire. Magnets hung like awkward beads amid crystals of midnight onyx and grey feldspar.

"It is a subtle stimulation," he murmured. "And certainly Love is not a subtle energy. But given sufficient time, it will work."

He directed that Zuleika sit in a chair in the parlor without disturbing the netting for three days.

The days passed slowly. Zuleika kept her eyes fixed on the window, which framed a cloudless, sunless, skyless world. She could feel the magnetic energies pulling her thoughts this way and that, but it seemed to her things remained much the same overall.

On the third day, the rat appeared.

"My beautiful fiancée," it said, gazing at where she sat. "What is that thing you wear?"

"It is a mechanism to remove Love," she said.

Its whiskers perked forward, and it looked pleased. "So you are in love?"

"No," she said. "But my father believes that I am."

"Hmmph," said the rat. "Tell me, what is the effect of such a mechanism if you are not in love?"

"I don't know."

It considered, absently flicking its tail.

"Perhaps it will have the opposite effect," it said.

"I have been thinking about that myself," she said. "Indeed, I feel fonder towards you with every passing moment."

"How much longer must you wear it?"

Her eyes sought the clock. "Another hour," she said.

"Then we must wait and see." The rat sniffed the air. "Did your family have muffins again this morning?"

"I've been sitting here for three days; I didn't have breakfast."

"Then I shall be back within a half hour or so," it said and withdrew.

At the hour, the door opened, and her father and the Physician entered. The rat, licking its chops, discreetly moved beneath her chair where, hidden by her skirts, it could not be seen.

"Well, my daughter," her father said, patting her on the back as the Physician removed the apparatus. "Do you feel restored?"

"Indeed I do," she said.

"Good, good!" He clapped the Physician's shoulder, looking pleased. "Good work, man. Shall we retire to discuss your fee?"

The Physician looked at Zuleika. "Perhaps another examination . . . " he ventured.

"No need," her father said briskly. "Love removed, everything's fixed. Our city can continue on as it has for the past millennium."

When they had gone, the rat crept out from beneath her chair, regarding her. "Well?" it said.

"I do not wish to be married down here."

"We can make our way to the surface and say our vows in Tabat," the rat said. "I know all the tunnels, and where they wind to."

And so she took a lantern from where it hung in the garden, shedding its dim light over the pale vegetation nourished there by sorcery rather than sunlight. They made their way to the first tunnel entrance, the rat riding on her shoulder, and started towards the surface. Behind them, there came a massive crash and crack.

"What was that?" the rat said.

"Nothing," Zuleika said. "Nothing at all, anymore."

She marched on and behind her, the city with no name continued to fall.

The Farmer's Cat
Jeff VanderMeer

A long time ago, in Norway, a farmer found he had a big problem with trolls. Every winter, the trolls would smash down the door to his house and make themselves at home for a month. Short or tall, fat or thin, hairy or hairless, it didn't matter—every last one of these trolls was a disaster for the farmer. They ate all of his food, drank all of the water from his well, guzzled down all of his milk (often right from the cow!), broke his furniture, and farted whenever they felt like it.

The farmer could do nothing about this—there were too many trolls. Besides, the leader of the trolls, who went by the name of Mobhead, was a big brute of a troll with enormous claws who emitted a foul smell from all of the creatures he'd eaten raw over the years. Mobhead had a huge, gnarled head that seemed green in one kind of light and purple in another. Next to his head, his body looked shrunken and thin, but despite the way they looked his legs were strong as steel; they had to be or his head would have long since fallen off of his neck.

"Don't you think you'd be more comfortable somewhere else?" the farmer asked Mobhead during the second winter. His wife and children had left him for less troll-infested climes. He had lost a lot of his hair from stress.

"Oh, I don't think so," Mobhead said, cleaning his fangs with a toothpick made from a sharpened chair leg. The chair in question had been made by the farmer's father many years before.

"No," Mobhead said. "We like it here just fine." And farted to punctuate his point.

Behind him, one of the other trolls devoured the family cat, and belched.

The farmer sighed. It was getting hard to keep help, even in the summers, when the trolls kept to their lairs and caves far to the north. The farm's reputation had begun to suffer. A few more years of this and he would have to sell the farm, if any of it was left to sell.

Behind him, one of the trolls attacked a smaller troll. There was a splatter of blood against the far wall, a smell oddly like violets, and then the severed head of the smaller troll rolled to a stop at the farmer's feet. The look on the dead troll's face revealed no hint of surprise.

Nor was there a look of surprise on the farmer's face.

All spring and summer, the farmer thought about what he should do. Whether fairly or unfairly, he was known in those parts for thinking his way out of every problem that had arisen during twenty years of running the farm. But he couldn't fight off the trolls by himself. He couldn't bribe them to leave. It worried him almost as much as the lack of rain in July.

Then, in late summer, a traveling merchant came by the farm. He stopped by twice a year, once with pots, pans, and dried goods and once with livestock and pets. This time, he brought a big, lurching wooden wagon full of animals, pulled by ten of the biggest, strongest horses the farmer had ever seen.

Usually, the farmer bought chickens from the tall, mute merchant, and maybe a goat or two. But this time, the merchant pointed to a cage that held seven squirming, chirping balls of fur. The farmer looked at them for a second, looked away, then looked again, more closely, raising his eyebrows.

"Do you mean to say . . ." the farmer said, looking at the tall, mute merchant. "Are you telling me . . ."

The mute man nodded. The frown of his mouth became, for a moment, a mischievous smile.

The farmer smiled. "I'll take one. One should be enough."

The mute man's smile grew wide and deep.

That winter, the trolls came again, in strength—rowdy, smelly, raucous, and looking for trouble. They pulled out a barrel of his best beer and drank it all down in a matter of minutes. They set fire to his attic and snuffed it only when Mobhead bawled them out for "crapping where you eat, you idiots!"

They noticed the little ball of fur curled up in a basket about an hour after they had smashed down the front door.

"Ere now," said one of the trolls, a foreign troll from England, "Wot's this, wot?"

One of the other trolls—a deformed troll, with a third eye protruding like a tube from its forehead—prodded the ball of fur with one of its big clawed toes. "It's a cat, I think. Just like the last one. Another juicy, lovely cat."

A third troll said, "Save it for later. We've got plenty of time."

The farmer, who had been watching all of this, said to the trolls, "Yes, this is our new cat. But I'd ask that you not eat him. I need him around to catch mice in the summer or when you come back next time, I won't have any grain, and no grain means no beer. It also means lots of other things won't be around for you to eat, like that homemade bread you seem to enjoy so much. In fact, I might not even be around, then, for without grain this farm cannot survive."

The misshapen troll sneered. "A pretty speech, farmer. But don't worry about the mice. We'll eat them all before we leave."

So the farmer went to Mobhead and made Mobhead promise that he and his trolls would leave the cat alone.

"Remember what you said to the trolls who tried to set my attic on fire, O Mighty Mobhead," the farmer said, in the best tradition of flatterers everywhere.

Mobhead thought about it for a second, then said, "Hmmm. I must admit I've grown fond of you, farmer, in the way a wolf is fond of a lamb. And I do want our winter resort to be in good order next time we come charging down out of the frozen north. Therefore, although I have this nagging feeling I might regret this, I will let you keep the cat. But everything else we're going to eat, drink, ruin, or fart on. I just want to make that clear."

The farmer said, "That's fine, so long as I get to keep the cat."

Mobhead said he promised on his dead mothers' eyeteeth, and then he called the other trolls around and told them that the cat was off limits. "You are not to eat the cat. You are not to taunt the cat. You must leave the cat alone."

The farmer smiled a deep and mysterious smile. It was the first smile for him in quite some time. A troll who swore on the eyeteeth of his mothers could never break that promise, no matter what.

And so the farmer got to keep his cat. The next year, when the trolls came barging in, they were well into their rampage before they even saw the cat. When they did, they were a little surprised at how big it had grown. Why, it was almost as big as a dog. And it had such big teeth, too.

"It's one of those Northern cats," the farmer told them. "They grow them big up there. You must know that, since you come from up there. Surely you know that much?"

"Yes, yes," Mobhead said, nodding absent-mindedly, "we know that, farmer," and promptly dove face-first into a large bucket of offal.

But the farmer noticed that the cat made the other trolls nervous. For one thing, it met their gaze and held it, almost as if it weren't an animal, or thought itself their equal. And it didn't really look like a cat, even a Northern cat, to them. Still, the farmer could tell that the other trolls didn't want to say anything to their leader. Mobhead liked to eat the smaller trolls because they were, under all the hair, so succulent, and none of them wanted to give him an excuse for a hasty dinner.

Another year went by. Spring gave on to the long days of summer, and the farmer found some solace in the growth of not only his crops but also his cat. The farmer and his cat would take long walks through the fields, the farmer teaching the cat as much about the farm as possible. And he believed that the cat even appreciated some of it.

Once more, too, fall froze into winter, and once more the trolls came tumbling into the farmer's house, led by Mobhead. Once again, they trashed the place as thoroughly as if they were roadies for some drunken band of Scandinavian lute players.

They had begun their second trashing of the house, pulling down the cabinets, splintering the chairs, when suddenly they heard a growl that turned their blood to ice and set them to gibbering, and at their rear there came the sound of bones being crunched, and as they turned to look and see what was happening, they were met by the sight of some of their friends being hurled at them with great force.

The farmer just stood off to the side, smoking his pipe and chuckling from time to time as his cat took care of the trolls. Sharp were his fangs! Long were his claws! Huge was his frame!

Finally, Mobhead walked up alongside the farmer. He was so shaken, he could hardly hold up his enormous head.

"I could eat you right now, farmer," Mobhead snarled. "That is the largest cat I have ever seen—and it is trying to kill my trolls! Only *I* get to kill my trolls!"

"Nonsense," the farmer said. "My cat only eats mice. Your trolls aren't mice, are they?"

"I eat farmers sometimes," Mobhead said. "How would you like that?"

The farmer took the pipe out of his mouth and frowned. "It really isn't up to me. I don't think Mob-Eater would like that, though."

"Mob-Eater?"

"Yes—that's my name for my cat."

As much as a hairy troll can blanch, Mobhead blanched exactly that much and no more.

"Very well, I won't eat you. But I *will* eat your hideous cat," Mobhead said, although not in a very convincing tone.

The farmer smiled. "Remember your promise."

Mobhead scowled. The farmer knew the creature was thinking about breaking his promise. But if he did, Mobhead would be tormented by nightmares in which his mothers tortured him with words and with deeds. He would lose all taste for food. He would starve. Even his mighty head would shrivel up. Within a month, Mobhead would be dead . . .

Mobhead snarled in frustration. "We'll be back when your cat is gone, farmer," he said. "And then you'll pay!"

If he'd had a cape instead of a dirty pelt of fur-hair, Mobhead would have whirled it around him as he left, trailing the remains of his thoroughly beaten and half-digested trolls behind him.

"You haven't heard the last of me!" Mobhead yowled as he disappeared into the snow, now red with the pearling of troll blood.

The next winter, Mobhead and his troll band stopped a few feet from the farmer's front door.

"Hey, farmer, are you there?!" Mobhead shouted.

After a moment, the door opened wide and there stood the farmer, a smile on his face.

"Why, Mobhead. How nice to see you. What can I do for you?"

"You can tell me if you still have that damn cat. I've been looking forward to our winter get-away."

The farmer smiled even more, and behind him rose a huge shadow with large yellow eyes and rippling muscles under a thick brown pelt. The claws on the shadow were big as carving knives, and the fangs almost as large.

"Why, yes," the farmer said, "as it so happens I still have Mob-Eater. He's a very good mouser."

Mobhead's shoulders slumped.

It would be a long hard slog back to the frozen north, and only troll to eat along the way. As he turned to go, he kicked a small troll out of his way.

"We'll be back next year," he said over his shoulder. "We'll be back every year until that damn cat is gone."

"Suit yourself," the farmer said, and closed the door.

Once inside, the farmer and the bear laughed.

"Thanks, Mob-Eater," the farmer said. "You looked really fierce."

The bear huffed a deep bear belly laugh, sitting back on its haunches in a huge comfy chair the farmer had made for him.

"I am really fierce, father," the bear said. "But you should have let me chase them. I don't like the taste of troll all that much, but, oh, I do love to chase them."

"Maybe next year," the farmer said. "Maybe next year. But for now, we have chores to do. I need to teach you to milk the cows, for one thing."

"But I hate to milk the cows," the bear said. "You know that."

"Yes, but you still need to know how to do it, son."

"Very well. If you say so."

They waited for a few minutes until the trolls were out of sight, and then they went outside and started doing the farm chores for the day.

Soon, the farmer thought, his wife and children would come home, and everything would be as it was before. Except that now they had a huge talking bear living in their house.

Sometimes folktales didn't end quite the way you thought they would. But they *did* end.

A Key Decides its Destiny

Cat Rambo

Because Solon DesCant was the greatest enchanter of his time, which spanned centuries, Lily had chosen him for a teacher despite the peril. He had produced wonders for the Duke of Tabat, performed miracles for the Emperor, and even vanished mysteriously for a decade, returning to claim he had undertaken certain unpalatable tasks for the demons of S'Keral.

Every fifty years Solon took an apprentice, whose work was to straighten the shelves of his workroom, to fetch and carry, cook and clean, tend his chickens, and run errands beneath the magician's dignity. In return he taught the apprentice the ins and outs of enchanting and the secrets he had spent his life discovering. And sometime in the forty-ninth year, Solon would kill the apprentice before they could carry his secrets out into the world. Two had escaped this fate by fleeing before that year arrived. But the final year was the year of true knowledge and many had let their thirst for secrets keep them there until it was too late and they found death in one of the ingenious poisons of which Solon was master.

Today's creation was a minor magic. He made the key out of cats' whiskers braided together and hardened with the chill from a heart that has never known love. He couldn't resist embellishment so he carved roses from mouse bone and attached the beads on strands of lignum vitae. Handling it required care – whisker tips protruded along its length like tiny thorns and a drop of blood swelled on his finger where one pricked him. The manticores stuffed and mounted on the walls of his workroom watched him with glassy eyes as he held it up.

"Is that it?" Lily asked from the doorway. He nodded, setting the key down on the table so they both could study it. She tucked her hands behind her back as she looked at it like a child examining a fragile heirloom, afraid of breaking it.

"What will it unlock?"

He shrugged. "Enchanted keys choose what they will unlock. But I've made this for the Witch, who hopes to persuade it to the destiny she prefers." He wrapped the key in a length of velvet before handing it to the apprentice. "Lily, you'll take this to her. There will be no payment; I'll ask her for a favor in due time."

She chewed her lip at the thought, looking down at the bundle.

"You'll have to learn to deal with witches at some point," he said. He reached for an alembic and pulled it in front of him, readying his next experiment. "It might as well be now."

"Is there anything I need to know beforehand?" she asked.

"Don't look in her eyes and be polite above all else. Witches take offense very easily."

Lily went down the winding stone stairs. The thought of delivering to the witch made her dizzy with nerves – witches are uncanny sorts and dangerous to cross. Girding herself with charms and amulets to fortify her courage, she slung a cloak around her shoulders, dark as night, soft as a smile, and went down the road towards the Thornwoods. She hunted up and down the paths, stepping right and left, walking deosil rather than risk the bad luck of widdershins, and trying to ignore the boggarts that hunted through the branches, watching her with sly eyes like cracks of light in a darkened room.

The key rested heavily in her pocket. A key that could open any door if it were persuaded. It burned in her mind like Magnesia Alba, which ignites hot and white when exposed to the air.

The witch lived in a cavern. Two great beasts crouched on either side of its entrance, mawed like panthers, tailed like scorpions. The apprentice did not look at them directly but she could feel their eyes like flames against her back as she walked down into the darkness.

The air was cold on her face and the plink of falling moisture echoed in the distance. Once something small and leathery-winged flapped past but she pressed on.

Up ahead an archway held the warmth of torchlight and through it was the witch's chamber, unexpectedly cheerful. Rugs woven in scarlet and purple covered the rocky floor, swallowing Lily's footsteps. The witch sat at a table, laying down cards made of stiff paper and painted in elaborate detail, colored with powdered lapis lazuli and gold leaf.

The witch did not look up until the last card had been laid down. Then finally she raised her gaze.

"You're new," she said. "Got you running errands, does he?"

"I've brought the key you wanted made."

"Have you now? Let me see it."

A touch of reluctance slowing her movements, Lily put the velvet bundle in the witch's hands. She unwrapped it like a long-awaited present, her eyes gleaming with avarice.

"I'll lift a curse with this," she gloated, fondling the haft and ignoring its tiny thorns. She frowned as it twisted in her grasp. "What's this? This key has already decided its purpose – one that is no good to me."

"I brought it straight from Solon's hands," Lily said, bewildered.

Drawing back her arm, the witch flung the key in Lily's direction. It glanced across her cheek, drawing blood as it hit and fell without a sound to the carpet. "Take it back and tell Solon I demand a new one within the next century."

Shaking with fear, Lily picked up the key and put it back in her pocket. She moved to retrieve the scrap of velvet but the witch motioned her away. "Be off and be glad I don't set the blood in your veins to boiling! It's you I blame for the key's decision."

The trip back through the corridors seemed longer than it had going down but at last she saw the light of the entrance and made her way out. A beast snapped at her, rending her cloak, but she hurried on.

Back at the tower she hesitated at the foot of the stairs. Solon's temper was slow to rise but fierce as a dragon's blaze when awakened. She wavered on the bottom step, slipping a hand into her pocket. The thorns stung her and she thought, *Why bring pain upon myself now? He won't know until he asks the witch for a favor, and that may be centuries away.* She turned and went to the workroom to grind sulfur crystals into the fine powder that summoning spells demand. Distracted by the demands of constructing a matrix for water elementals, Solon never asked about her errand.

Days passed and the key remained in her pocket. At night she puzzled over what its purpose might be – if she and Solon were the only people who had touched it before the witch then it must be shaped to the desires of one or the other of them. *If it is Solon's, it could be anything,* she thought, *but after all he took precautions and great care in shaping it. He must, after all, know the best way to prevent such things.*

Perhaps it's my desire that gave it purpose, she thought. *The witch did say she blamed me. Perhaps it is the key to Solon's heart.* She fell into daydreams of romance where Solon declared his passion and vowed to lay the world at her feet, where he slew hippogriffs and kings for her and built a castle of rose-colored crystal on the slopes of Berzul, the dwarf-infested mountain that is the tallest in the world.

Yes, he'll love me, she thought. *He will be unable to kill the woman he loves.* She began to watch him for signs of passion: sighs or glances, or uncharacteristic lapses into poetry. Sometimes she thought she glimpsed warmth in his eyes as he demonstrated how to dissect a basilisk and preserve its delicate, fan-shaped heart or as he leaned over her to show the steady back and forth of the pestle necessary to produce a diamond powder as fine as flour, tiny glittering particles floating in the air around the mortar, falling onto the sheet of parchment Solon had placed on the table to catch them.

But there was nothing certain as the years passed and finally Lily thought, *He's waiting until I am no longer his apprentice, but his equal, before he approaches me. How just of him! For he knows that otherwise I'd be distracted from my learning.*

And learn she did.

In the twentieth year of her apprenticeship, she learned to tie time in a loop to keep herself from aging; in the twenty-fifth year, how to weave moonlight and sunlight together in a rope that neither creatures of the day nor creatures of the night could escape. In the thirtieth year, Solon showed her how to make a saddle that could sit any steed, from dragon to crocodile, and more. At night the knowledge dancing in her head kept her from sleeping and she took to midnight walks around the tower roof, walking in circles until the cloud of facts settled, sifting into layer upon layer in her mind.

In the fortieth year she became aware that Solon watched her covertly, gazing when he thought she would not notice. It confirmed her hopes and she took to wearing fripperies and furbelows, making sure her shirt fit snugly, and putting belladonna in her eyes to make them shine.

As the forty-ninth year approached, Solon taught her more and more and praised her for her quickness. "No apprentice has ever taken to things so swiftly," he told her and she glowed with happiness.

The beginning of the year came and went. Lily took simple precautions such as checking her food and drink with a unicorn's horn because she did not want Solon to think her stupid or that she knew his secret love. The moment that he announced it would be all the sweeter if he thought she did not know. She imagined it over and over again, wondering how he would choose to tell her, picturing his handsome face creased with worry that she might not reciprocate. She was pleased to see that he took over more of the work that she had previously performed, such as preparing his morning meal and doing his laundry. *Getting used for the rearrangement of the household when I become his wife*, she thought.

On a day that dawned clear and bright Solon asked her into his workroom. *Now*, she thought, *he'll tell me now*. He stood framed by the sunlight coming in the window, gazing at her. She gathered her skirts and took a chair.

"I regret to tell you," Solon said, still looking at her. "that you will be dead by tomorrow. The laundry soap has had a poison in it for the last two weeks—I calculated it to match your body weight and allow it to cumulate into a dose sufficient to end your apprenticeship at midnight. Give or take a half hour."

She looked at him, horrified. Her fingers played over the key in her pocket. "But you love me," she protested.

He looked surprised. "Dear child, where would you have gotten that idea? I am sworn to celibacy for the sake of my art."

68

The thorns on the key pricked and stung her but they were not the source of the blood warm tears rolling down her face. She felt the key stir beneath her touch and finally realized its purpose.

And when she plunged it into his heart, piercing it as love could not, he was as surprised as she had been, dying with a startled look fixed on his lean and timeless face.

She went downstairs and put her things in order, tidying the shelves and sweeping the floor one last time. She dusted the tall glass jars of powders and set the flock of chickens loose, shooing them away. Then she went to sit on the tower roof, listening to the owl's call, and waited for midnight to arrive.

Three Sons

Cat Rambo

Once upon a time, there was a minor official of the desert city of Allanak. His name was Arylian, and he was altogether an unremarkable man, destined to remain in his blue robe of rank, and whose only moment of note had been a conversation with Garrick of the Red.

Some of his lack of remarkableness he had brought on himself, for he was a quiet man, and not given to flamboyant gestures or clever conversations. And his quietness did not reflect any sort of profound or philosophical ruminations, but was the quiet of a man who took life as it presented itself, with little wonder or appreciation. His appearance made up the other part of his lack of remarkableness, for he was, like most of the inhabitants of Allanak, dark of skin, hair, and eyes, and not overly tall.

The life of an official has certain bonuses, such as the ability to tax people at whim, or to confiscate spice or coins or concubines, but with those benefits come certain perils, such as assassination attempts by disgruntled merchants or fellow officials. After Arylian had seen the third of his fellows dead to poison or a quick knife, he decided he would avoid suffering the same fate by hiring guards. Good guards, loyal guards. And to this matter, he lent a certain amount of thought and, at length, arrived at an idea.

He went to the slaving house of Borsail, and told the slave keeper that he wished to purchase three ogres, of a very young age. Old enough to walk, but not old enough to speak clearly.

And when he had made his selection among the array of the best that Borsail had to offer, he went home with his new charges toddling after him.

For Arylian was clever enough when need held, and he had decided that the best ties are those of blood, or believed blood, and that if the ogres believed he was related to them, they would serve him gladly enough. So he set about convincing them, over the next few years, that he was their father.

"Look!" he told the ogres, who he had named Tug and Toby and Teracitus, as he touched his face. "Just like me, you have two eyes. You inherited those from me, your father! And two ears, and a nose, though mine is a trifle longer than yours. This is how I know you are my sons, and I love you well, just as you love me, your father."

And the ogres, who were as simpleminded as any other of their breed, nodded and accepted his word. As they grew older, he dressed them in armor, and had them trained to fight, and wherever he went, his three ogres trailed after him, solemnly following their sire.

There were uncomfortable questions at times, such as the fate of the trio's mother, but Arylian concocted a story of a beautiful ogress, with long dark hair that fell to her ankles, who had come from the shores of the Sea of Silt to fall in love with him, and who had died to an assassin attempting to kill him. The story grew over time and by the end, Arylian was half in love with his creation, whose eyes were blue, and lips were full, and who had a cleverer turn of mind than most of the larger humanoids. And every once in a while, Tug or Toby might slip, and call him father in public, but he discouraged that, pointing out that if assassins knew they were his beloved sons, they might kill the ogres as they had killed their mother, attempting to cause the police official pain.

On a hot day, when dust cloaked the streets and the beggars fought over the slightest sliver of shade, Arylian and his ogres went out walking. They paced the length of Meleth's Circle, and along Caravan Road. Near the gates, where the crowds were thickest, Arylian felt someone tug at his belt pouch, and turned in time to see a lean, wiry pickpocket tucking away the stolen pouch with one long fingered hand.

"Seize him!" he shouted, pointing at the thief. The ogres did.

The thief pleaded for mercy, words spilling from his lips faster than sand grains being swept across a dune, and Arylian frowned and scowled and refused to listen. Telling Tug to continue holding onto the thief, he went in search of a collar and whip, for he meant to flay the man's skin from his bones, and enslave him for daring to touch Arylian's person.

And so the thief continued speaking, trying to persuade the ogres to let him go, in the name of kindness, and mercy, and various other qualities. But Tug and Toby and Tericatus all sadly shook their immense shaggy heads.

"Father wouldn't like that," Tug said and the thief paused and looked at him, astonished.

"Father?" he said.

Tericatus pointed in the direction that Arylian had taken, and all three nodded their heads.

"How," said the thief, the words as slow as his thoughts were fast, "How could such a thing come to be?"

Tug leaned to whisper in his ear. "It is a long story. But he is our father. For proof of this, you have but to look at us, for do we not have two eyes, just as he does? And do we not have one mouth, and one nose, just as he?"

The thief's face cleared. "Ah!" he said. "My luck has turned. For here I came to Allanak, myself, searching for my three long lost brothers. Perhaps you've seen them? They are ogres, all fierce and brave, and each one of them has two eyes, and but a single nose . . . "

Astonished, the three gaped at him and then one by one, they extended their arms and hugged him tightly, each shouting "Brother!" to the great astonishment of the passersby.

And when Arylian returned carrying his whip, and a collar, he found his ogres gone. The thief had persuaded them to come wandering with him, and where he led them, and where their bones lie, those three sons, no one knows to this day.

The Strange Case of the Lovecraft Café
M. F. Korn, D. F. Lewis, Jeff VanderMeer

Dear Malik Sultan:

I am rushed for time, but will attempt to put what I know into perspective, since I did promise to in my last missive. Excuse a certain terseness, which I know to be at odds with my usual languorous approach . . .

After only three months of serving gourmet foods to its selective clientele, the "Lovecraft Café" (my moniker for it, for it remained Nameless during its brief existence on this Earth) perished in a fire that appears to have no salient cause. While arson cannot be ruled out, neither can it be ruled in. The proprietor, a Mr. Ward—who, by all accounts, appeared to the local populace as half-lifeless flotsam amongst the ruins of a rudderless old-fashioned wooden ship borne hard-up against the local reef—cannot be found, nor were his remains discovered on the property.

In the charred wreckage, however, the would-be rescuers first to the scene did uncover several strange skeletons that possessed long, twisted spines and no arm bones. It is supposed that these remains were mere life-like models of outré creatures, but forensic results have proven ambivalent on this score.

Town officials are at a loss—even more so because it appears the Café operated without the appropriate licenses for its short lifespan. Why the various and sundry inspectors that prey off such towns like blood-engorged ticks did not become aware of

this situation for such a lengthy period is unknown.

Meanwhile, patrons give conflicting reports not only with regard to what lured them to the Café, but also as to what befell them whilst frequenting it. For it would appear that several patrons left the Café in a mutilated but cauterized, or *surgically healed*, form. Despite these rather extreme alterations, not a one leveled any complaint or even a scurrilous rumor about the Café. Indeed, police found two of the disfigured patrons wailing plaintively at the edges of the smoldering ruins after the conflagration. When questioned, it became apparent that both individuals had frequented the Café even *after* their transformative experiences.

Asked by the local constabulary as to why he would dare return to the very place where he had become so mutilated, one of the patrons reportedly and repeatedly replied, "I heard a strange an' ethereal music. I heard a strange an' ethereal music," followed by the strange syntax of "*Which dishes be these that bleat so beatifically?*"

Subsequent encounters with other patrons suggest that the combination of ambiance and food in the Café had a profound effect.

"There shall gelatinous be our fate under the roilsome seas, and we shall take to it blissfully," one individual said.

"One plank, I say, one spoonful, one syrupping of their pearling bed I long to be, consumed by time and wormwood," said another.

The possibility of some kind of hypnosis or *untoward suggestion* or *mass hallucination* cannot be ruled out, although various head physicians have yet to make a determination in that regard. As to my own speculations upon the subject, I have begun to wonder if the dishes served at the cafe were, in an odd and succulent way, a gateway—to another plane of experience, perhaps even to that Place we must never name?

Another, melodramatically precise, transcript from an "eye-witness," provides some insight into what may have happened to the establishment (I managed to retrieve this, undetected, from the headquarters of the local embodiment of the law):

> "Fer the likes a me, I din't see nothin' but a blue whis-tlin' flame on 'it, I tell 'ya . . . I w's scear'd silly . . . I tell ya, that place burnt down quiet lak a lit'l baby 'cept fer that whist'lin sound. 'Ah tell 'ya, the blue flame were 'a drawin' me to it' lak ' a moth t' a flame!"
> —Alan Brown, farmer

I must confess to discovering very little of use in official sources, such as the local broadsheets, although digging back a few months, I did stumble across an odd paragraph buried in a polemic otherwise mostly given over to an unfavorable dissec-tion of local cuisine.

> Chef K Paul Antoine noted that a mysteriously swarthy dwarf-sized gentleman with stentorian breathing and cloaked in swaddling Tibetan cloth had recently given notice as soucier chef at Galatoires, a famous restaurant that Faulkner used to visit during the 1920s, and his last words to one of his confidant busboys was, "There will be a whole swarm of them coming through! . . . I've got the black book! Yog Suthoth!"

I then conducted a thorough search of the area around the burned down Café, although, alas, the presence of the Law made it impossible to search the Café itself. The only evidence I found were a few charred fragments of the Café's menu, and what appears to be some sort of diary entry, each shred of which I attach to this letter for your bemusement. (A bribe to a certain sergeant gave me the luxury of a photocopy.)

These fragments appear lacking in any clues relevant to what you seek, although many of the details will be of intense interest, perhaps even worthy of a raised eyebrow. The last fragment (the "diary" entry) may have been part of the menu, as it is printed on the same paper and uses the same font, although employing a different color of ink. Should it be so, I can only assume this element constituted an informational part of the menu, perhaps dealing with the brief history of the Café?

I should note the strange properties of these fragments, regardless of their relevance or irrelevance. I found them trapped beneath the incoherent remains of several evil-looking black-skinned book spines, the text within long since fallen to siege by flame, and when I first pulled them out from beneath their random tombstones, the menu text slipped in and out of focus like darting fish, before seeming to reconstitute itself into more familiar letters. This has not happened since, although I did find myself catching a sudden movement from the corner of my eye once or twice. I am sure it is just a symptom of my advancing age, but as is the way with me I find no detail too small to be of use.

It is my most sincere wish that I have relinquished unto you enough exploration and further mysteries to warrant your continued funding of my investigative work, since I find your ongoing quest of much more interest and enlightenment than the pursuit of more sordid, mundane inquiries.

I remain as always,
Yr Most oblig'd and Humble Servant,

Crawford Tillinghast

P.S. I must warn you not to peruse the menu items for very long at any one sitting. Otherwise you may, as have I, feel the compulsion to create these dishes, and down that path, I fear, lies our complete and utter ruination.

. . . . . .

SEAFOOD

"I cannot think of the deep sea without shuddering at the nameless things that may at this very moment be crawling & floundering on its slimy bed."

Crustaceans A La Hodgson — A sumptuous dish rendered by tossing undistressed winged crustaceans that have Fallen here to our mote dust globule from vectorless vortices of unplumbed galactic space into a large iron pot of steaming parboiling rainwater. Served hot with garlic butter and plenty of napkins. *Note:* Very hard to unshell but worth the effort.

Bleating Fresh Oyster-Catchers — The name speaks for itself. These undersea creatures known for their enlarged and oblong gullets are grilled to perfection over a hickory fire after being marinated in a mixture of herbs, wine and garlic for two days. Our staff will imitate the Bleaters famous lonesome love call when we bring them sizzling to your table.

Cuttlefish Des Goules — This delicacy is not for the Mundane Palette. According to legend, the Ghouls of Eurasia oft neglected their duties of grave robbing when the cuttlefish harvest came in. Although the small fish can be too bitter for some, we braise them in a sweet marinara paste and the results speak for themselves! Served with a choice of baked yam or stuffed potato.

FUNGI

"*. . . mound-like tentacles groping from underground nuclei of polypous perversion . . . insane lightning over malignant ivied walls and demon arcades choked with fungous vegetation . . .*"

Fungi Et Fruits De Mer (when in season) — A delight from the quaint town of Innsmouth. Rare New England fungi found seaside only when offshore jetties appear during the Innsmouth sea-bearing mating season. Fishermen manage each year to avert their eyes from the prurient interbreeding of Mortals and their Cousins from the Deep as these brave men and women scoop up gallons of this delectable delicacy worth its gastronomical weight in gold. Kept in oak casks for years for aging, it is then prepared in a mouth-watering vegetable custard, garnished with sea cucumber florets and topped with lump crabmeat.

. . .

Pan-Tossed Nemonymi From Yuggoth — These delicate rare fungal tastes from the Lost Atlantis of our deepest unknown cellar are baked for months between specially made clay brickbats. However, for optimum tenderization and to trigger their true toothsome Yuggoth flavor, they will be lightly tossed by your table in red-hot woks of evaporating apricot juice. The hissing scream emitted thereby is simply a byproduct of the steam, not, as some have supposed, a final death cry.

. . .

unnamable uneatables tenderized in Moon Bog stew with tasty gristle back-bite

. . .

Dark Peabodies Whitened In The Vault — These long sausage delicacies (unique to our menu) come already copper-bottomed—i.e. still sewn into the vessels where they were cooked—the awesome flavor being retained and securely brought to the dining table by this revolutionary method. We provide special pinking-scissors for cutting the sewing-thread (and indeed the porous yet strong sausage-skin itself). The very act of the diner thus "shelling" the peabodies enhances the full culinary experience of taste, smell, and mastication.

. . .

FOWL

"Poultry turned greyish and died very quickly, their meat being found dry and noisome upon cutting."

De Vermis Mysteriis — This rare dish comes from the book of its name and there have been many variations throughout the ages. Our award-winning recipe (perhaps the most guarded secret of our establishment) puts an end to that. The poultry chef is an expert at Ancient Aramaic and sorcery runs in the family; one must read the preamble to the Occult tome before the chicken is cut up and sautéed in a red curry tai sauce with orange zest, lemon and ginger. Add chicken stock and andouille sausage. Served over rice in a bowl or cup.

Flaming Whole Giant Penguin — Served flaming in its entirety, from beak to excavated bowels (filled with smaller fowl such as whole marinated quail, owls, and dwarf eagles), and recently retrieved for your eating pleasure from the Mountains of Madness, the bird is first plucked, the feathers replaced in a more aesthetically pleasing pattern. A delightful concoction of fat, pounded ham, offal, spices, prunes, dried sour cherries, cheese, and eggs is injected under the fat layer. The whole is then alternately slow-roasted on a spit and placed on mounds of melting ice to preserve the glacial allure of the living bird. *Note:* We require three days' advance notice to capture and prepare this dish for you.

. . .

Onion-stained unmentionables skewered on red hooks

. . .

SPECIALTY DISHES

" . . . *a loathsome night-spawned flood of organic corruption . . . seething, stewing, surging, bubbling like serpents's slime . . .* "

Darioles of Nethermost Blight in Black Being Sauce — A classic dish for which discerning gastronomes require no description.

Deep Fried Ones — For the truly hungry, a stick-to-the-ribs meal of glistening fried meat, fibrous yet gelid, served with old fashioned barbecue sauce or twenty-year-old balsamic vinaigrette. A side of squid larvae is highly recommended as the perfect complement to this dish.

From The Chef's Perspective [inset]

How to Prepare . . .

Deep Fried Ones — After deveining and deboning each One, soak whole in a large egg wash once; then coat with Louisiana Fish Fry (seasoned), then back in the egg wash, and back once again in the seasoned corn meal. Set for five minutes and in fryer (use only Beef Suet) for fifteen minutes until they float. Set aside to drain.

. . .

Lurking Fear Short Ribs — Recommended for the adventurous soul only. About this dish, our chef would divulge only a cryptic warning: "Swaddled in blankets, a whisperer in darkness with lobster-like claws and the wings of bats. Fetid odor as of the grave. There be short ribs, and there be short ribs." Once we receive the first order for this dish, it will be stricken from the menu.

Piping Hot Frogs — Only the largest bullfrogs from the nearby swamps are served in this dish, sautéed whole in onions, bell pepper, celery, shallots, woodears, and Chanterelles. After browning, a deglazing with mold jugged claret occurs, and a roux is formed from the drippings, with whole cream added. One ten-pound bullfrog serves two.

Potluck Fondue — A delightful variation on traditional fondue, with a potpourri of clawed and scaled surprises struggling for suzerainty in a pot of boiling oil flavored with spices of the orient. Use skewers to determine which perish and which survive long enough to be devoured, perfectly mirroring the context of the larger world.

. . .

DESSERTS

"Pie is my favourite dessert, and blueberry (for summer) and mince (for winter) are my preferred kinds—with apple as a good all-year-round third. Like to take vanilla ice cream with apple and blueberry pie." (from HPL to REH)

Dripping Eidolon — This dripping gathers the sweet creamy residues of roasting matured ectoplasm. Ghost or no, this pudding of a tangy consistency smells as good as it tastes. The sound it makes when sucked off of a spoon is akin to muffled moist noises made by flagellating a thousand spectral whippoorwills. Drizzled all over with spectral molasses.

Unknown Binding-Curds Milked From Nameless Kine In Kadath — Unknown, yes, but incredibly here to grace the plate: dressed in an alforja jacket, then oozed over with our well-known specialty blancmange as a bonus. We dare not divulge the true name of this dish for fear of transgressing the Unwritten Law of the yet unopened Tastebuds. After digesting these binding curds, you will find your glorious transformation complete, the intensity of the accompanying pain unimportant.

. . .

[diary fragment]

October 18 (entry the 7ᵗʰ)

My hands are trembling as I secretively set down this flailing missive which I know will be to no avail. No suitable ratiocination exists within my mindset and instrumentality of foul intemperance that can possibly assuage me in this dire hour. A shipmate, a Mrs. Tamar, came round to the bridge after we left that accursed port, which I shall not name, to alert the ship's captain of some sort of unnameable gelatinous hybrid creature that had brought on board for shippage to what I can only call the Foetid Establishment, supposedly suitable for use as sustenance for humans like myself and Mrs. Tamar. As the ship's chef, I did not agree. My training in the classical cuisine of the French and Italians did not include the Decadent Cookbook, I told them with some intensity. It seemed a point of some importance. I was told then that a mysteriously swarthed and notorious dwarf that had lashed himself to the fo'castle during a sudden invection of dramatic intensity while we lay becalmed in the Sargasso sea two days ago and shrieked "Yog Suthoth," had befriended this hideous foetid creature. It had, Mrs. Tamar informed us in the haughty tone that is her wont, been bred in the Jaywick area of Holland-by-Sea for slaughter by the Nymus Corporation, the founder, a man by the name of E.G. Lerch, the patriarch of a giant cottage industry of breeding old ones that got "stuck inbetwixt the dimensions," of which there was no escape but ulterior damage to internal organs of these monstrous gilled creatures, with seaweed-like hair, and this Lerch had connections of no unsimilar familiarity in the Narangansett port near Providence, namely local gentry of mongrelized haunch breeding and ill repute who ran the opium dens and sold Old Ones fur to the denizens and seamen who occupied the red light districts of said Providence. Lerch had been as good as his name in his ponderous journey up the barnacled ramp shore-side the first time I saw him. This stentorian breathing little dwarf never recognized anyone nor gave any salutation among the many friend sailors, but kept strangely to himself, and at our rare and halting dinners read a bizarre tome of some sort called something like THE NOMICON KITCHEN HELPER.

October 23 (entry the 8ᵗʰ)

I saw it in the lower decks. I saw it as led by Lerch and lurch it did, and whine it did, and clinging were its cringing undulations, leprous its malodorous bleating tendencies. Yet the two seemed to communicate one to the other, like the farmer conversing with the not-yet-slaughtered cow, butcher and butchered, chef and ingredients—and yet which was which? Lerch or Lurch? It was maggot-white and then whined into a Sargasso green, and it stank of every foul and rotting thing that ever died in three feet of water, choking on its own breath and vomit. How can I write this? Where shall I escape to? What shall I become? And when it turned, when it for a second turned and caught a hint of reflected moonlight cascaded and bounced from metal to wood down from the upper deck, I saw its thousand eyes and they were all turned on me, and Knew me.

October 30 (entry the last)

They are coming now after me, and much sooner than expected, for I had hoped for some respite to tell what must be told, but by now the whole of the crew has been slaughtered by forces unknown to this universe, lurching into ours by ways most foul. Mrs. Tamar has by means most devious departed/escaped from this ship, and what a bright and blinding light the portal made as it opened and as it closed! It was a sight to be savored as long as my eyes remain in my body. I had some early hope to regain control of the vessel as it is aimlessly adrift and entangled in the Sargasso Sea. However, this likelihood seems lessened by my current location hiding in a cupboard in the ship's galley, writing by surreptitious candle light. How I hate the words at my disposal, as they trip me with their complexity, break my fall only by sentence's end! And yet what to say? By now I write only to stop the gibbering from reaching my lips and putting an end to me by discovery. There are sounds padding slowly toward my safe place. There are footfalls on the ceiling of this floating room. Shall I survive this fey and foul putrefaction of the soul only to meet those thousand eyes and find myself the recipe not the receptor? Which dishes be these that bleat so beatifically yet stink of the nether places? I will put out this candle soon and find in that certain darkness . . .

Editor's Note: In checking the facts of this entire intercepted communication prior to this, its initial publication (the letter and accompanying documents found recently in a suddenly dead relative's moldering attic under some impressive 300-thread count sheets), we have it on good authority that Malik Sultan and Crawford Tillinghast met soon after these events. And, in contrast to the clandestine cast of their correspondence, met quite openly and, indeed, regularly, in a library not far from the remains of the café in question, thus risking their names being linked to the mystery they hoped to solve—or, dare we say, to the mystery *they may have actually brought about.*

However, madness comes in many forms, the deadliest of which takes the form of cumulative hearsays treated as the gospel truth. Indeed, there are many inscrutable and overlapping accounts of these meetings. For example, a nameless writer we tracked down in an equally nameless mental hospital was once irresponsibly allowed to make an unescorted visit to the library where he watched MS and CT through the wall of a neighboring carrel, his ears pricked to catch every word. Apparently, they shuffled books to hide what they said or chewed things that made their words tangle on their teeth. They spoke, however, unmistakably of under*things*, or under*people* who felt themselves of even lower grade than the ingredients in the recipes that MS and CT so yearned to fathom. The nameless earwigging writer scrawled in his notebook that "MS and CT also considered that such low life would have a greater pride and satisfaction in life if they could themselves be cooked and served still bleating to rich diners." Remaining uncooked was these sad creatures' only source of melancholy. The poor creatures surely yearned to be saucepanned or tandooried, claimed the eavesdropper on MS and CT's behalf.

Further, this source claimed that MS and CT, as well as menu exegetists, were the gang-masters facilitating nirvana for such under*things*-who-lusted-to-be-boiled-alive. But when the cafe fire intervened, the cover-up commenced with false trails, planted mysteries, concocted cookery-books, and doctored documents. Yet, by using interpretation rather than hearsay, we feel that confusion by fire is surely preferable to facing the music of organizing illegal labor—as often later discussed by MS and CT to each other through "mouthfuls of sweetly spiced backhanders upon a bed of mixed race" (a recriminatory quotation, it is deemed, from the nameless writer as filtered through his political motivation). We hasten to add that the already proliferating rumors that our unnamed unstable source is, in fact, the ageless Malik Sultan in disguise are baseless. It is more likely to be someone who wanted to muddy the waters of an otherwise clear-cut situation, given the propensity, in this day and age, to poeticize "primary sources" from a standpoint of deconstructive lunacy. Lay one transparent map of one place over another of another, and then whither do we go?

Author Notes

Two years ago, **Cat Rambo** threw caution to the winds and quit working as a mindless cog in the gears of a very large software corporation based in Seattle. A week later, she started Clarion West, studying with (alternately) Octavia Butler, Andy Duncan, L. Timmel Duchamp, Connie Willis, Gordon Van Gelder, and Michael Swanwick. Trapped in the confines of a sorority house surrounded by hooting frat boys, the sleep-deprived Clarion West students wrote a story a week and lived, breathed, and dreamed critiques of each other's work. It was not the first time Cat had been intensively writing, but it was the first time she was doing so under the banner of fantasy and science fiction. A decade earlier, she had received a master-of-arts degree from the Johns Hopkins Writing Seminars, where she'd written under the tutelage of John Barth and Steve Dixon, among others. It was there, as well as the experience of teaching Women's Studies at Towson State University, and later the Master's in English program at Indiana University, where she acquired a great deal of critical theory and promptly forgot half of it, while the rest would get buried in her brain and continue to inform her fiction. While at Hopkins, she'd written literary fiction that strayed into magic realism: Bigfoot being interviewed by the press, note-writing chickens, and talking dolls. The move to acknowledging her genre fiction roots was an easy and natural one, like opening a door and finding herself unexpectedly, mercifully at home.

Nine months ago, *Jeff VanderMeer* threw caution to the winds and quit working as a mindless cog in the gears of a fairly large software corporation based in Tallahassee. A week later, he was broke, but happily writing four or five mornings a week at Black Dog Cafe. He found his state of mind much improved and was able to collaborate for only the second time in his career, with Cat Rambo on "The Surgeon's Tale." He too had gone to Clarion, but to Clarion East, back in the early 1990s, where his instructors were James Patrick Kelly, Nancy Kress, a speaker phone with Harlan Ellison's voice rasping through it, Lisa Goldstein, Kate Wilheim, and Damon Knight. It was not the first time Jeff had been intensively writing, but it was near the beginning of doing so under the banner of fantasy and science fiction. In the 1980s, Jeff had edited a literary magazine and written poetry for mainstream literary journals, and established connections with the English and Creative Writing Faculty at the University of Florida. Jeff had dropped out of UF when he discovered journalism was not for him and all he wanted to do was write fiction. Since then, his fiction and editing interests have drifted into the surreal and magic realism. The move to acknowledging and combining his dual mainstream-genre roots has been like opening a door and trying to move through it while wearing roller skates that want to go off in different directions, and at the same time being pelted with praise and rotten tomatoes from all sides.

Artist Notes

Kris Dikeman, who did the interior art, lives and works in New York City. When she's not drawing pictures or designing books, she's writing. Her stories have appeared in the magazines *All Hallows* and *Sybil's Garage*. She's hard at work on her first novel, all about the invasion of Manhattan by hordes of brain-chomping zombies.

James A. Owen, who did the cover art and design, has been working professionally as an illustrator and storyteller for more than two decades. To date, in addition to numerous illustration and design projects, James has written and illustrated the six-volume *Essential Starchild* graphic novel series, and his novel *Here, There Be Dragons* was published by Simon & Schuster in the fall of 2006. At least six more books in the series are planned, and foreign rights have been sold in fourteen countries. James works at the Coppervale Studio, a 14,000 square foot, century-old restored church in Northeastern Arizona. For more information please go to http://www.coppervaleinternational.com or http://coppervale.livejournal.com/.

Once Upon a Time . . .

There was a surgeon with a terrible obsession
who befriended a dead girl in a strange underground city
from whence came the trolls that made the farmer's cat mad,
and which manifested itself on the surface in the form of both
the heart of a dark and sinister enchanter
and an eccentric, damned cafe.

No one lived happily ever after,
but some of them did, indeed, *live.*

The End

Printed in the United States
95779LV00001B/40-48/A

9 780809 572687